The Shoestringers

Benedict Trout, long-time foreman of the big K/K Ranch, has been cut loose for being too old, and Eddie Guest, a new-hire, has been fired for being too young. So with nowhere to go, Trout and Guest are riding west.

When they reach the RU Crooked Ranch they discover a place in terrible shape: run by a widow and her young daughter, the women are broke and without expectations. Standing at a crossroads, the ranch is coveted by the boss of a nearby town, Cyrus Sullivan, who is keen to investigate reports of a gold mine on the land.

The four unlikely allies are in this for the long haul, and must sit tight and fight long and hard to defend their shoestring operation against outlaws, thieves, and the greedy gold hunters.

By the same author

Ghost Ranch
Comes a Horseman
The Outlaw's Daughter
The Lonesome Death of Joe Savage
Climax
White Wind

The Shoestringers

C.J. Sommers

A Black Horse Western

ROBERT HALE · LONDON

ISBN 978-0-7198-1360-3

Robert Hale Limited
Clerkenwell House
Clerkenwell Green
London EC1R 0HT

www.halebooks.com

Typeset by
Derek Doyle & Associates, Shaw Heath
Printed and bound in Great Britain by
CPI Antony Rowe, Chippenham and Eastbourne

ONE

Long in the war, long on the range. Now what, long in the rocking chair? Not for Benjamin Trout, called Mr Benjamin by the younger hands on the K/K Ranch out of Waco, Texas where Trout had ridden for twenty years for Ed Kramer. Kramer had replaced Trout as foreman with a younger man. Paul Elliott was engaged to marry Kramer's daughter, Candice, so Trout could sort of understand the move, although it was a little humiliating.

What was unfathomable was that less than a month later Trout had been called into Kramer's office and told that his services were no longer required on the ranch.

'I don't want you to worry, though, Trout. You can stay on around the ranch helping out here and there. We'll offer you shelter and meals same as always. It's just that I won't be able to pay you anymore.'

'I'm not yet forty years old,' Benjamin Trout said. Age was the only reason he could think of for his dismissal.

'No, and you're still a tall, strong, good-looking man. You'd be in your prime in any other sort of job. You ought to give that some thought – another line of work, that is.'

'Mr Kramer, I know cows, horses, knots and brands, water sources, prairie medicine, Indians and guns. What other sort of work would you say I was suited for?'

Of course there was no answer to that and Kramer had apparently spent all of the time he intended to on Ben Trout.

'You have your options, Ben,' the ranch owner said. 'It's not like I'm throwing you out to the wolves. Stay or go as you please.'

'Then if it's all the same to you, Mr Kramer,' Benjamin said, rising from his chair, 'I'll be getting along.'

The coming sun was low outside the big house, the big oaks in the front yard still cast deep, cool shadows across the dusty earth.

The yardman, Connors, who was busy moving some rotted lumber from in front of the barn to a stack of discards, lifted his eyes and smiled as if to say something to Benjamin, but he must have seen something in Trout's eyes that stilled his greeting.

Trout walked on, hat tugged low against the rising sun, hearing the taunts and jeers, the familiar jokes of the crew as they saddled for their morning duties. These quieted a bit as Trout approached the bunkhouse. The word must have leaked out somehow. One of the men shouted out a 'Good morning, Mr Benjamin,' but Trout did not respond. He shuffled on, head down, toward the building he had called home for so many years on the K/K Ranch.

Inside the bunkhouse, someone was raising hell. Entering, Trout saw only two men. One was the camp cook, Frye, the other was a new-hire named Eddie Guest whom the hands had nicknamed 'Dink'. It was Dink who was causing the uproar. As Frye, a huge man in a white apron, watched, leaning against the wall, Dink went the length of the building throwing bedding, slats, coffee pots and cards on the floor, at the walls, his wild hair flying.

'Tantrum,' the taciturn Frye told Benjamin.

'What's going on here?' Trout demanded, halting Dink's unruly display of temper.

'What?' a panting Dink, hair limp across his eyes, bent forward at the waist, asked. 'You mean you don't know, Mr Benjamin? I got fired this

7

morning, that's what. Barely awake and they told me that I was fired, to pull my freight.'

'It happens. That's no reason to tear up the bunkhouse.'

'It's a reason,' Dink argued. He was no more than seventeen years old, just coming into his man's weight and strength. So far as Benjamin knew, his work was acceptable, although he made a few mistakes now and then. He had always seemed willing and content on the K/K.

'They didn't even give me a reason,' Dink went on complaining, as Benjamin walked to his own bunk to recover his few belongings. 'Folks call me "kid", but I do my best and I'm learning fast. Is that it, Mr Benjamin? Did they fire me because I'm too young?'

'I wouldn't know,' Trout said honestly. 'No one discussed it with me.'

'But, you're the foreman – you must have been told,' Dink said in disbelief. He wiped back his hair, glanced at Frye, who was straightening the kitchen chairs and the table, and then turned almost pleading eyes back toward Ben Trout.

'Couldn't you maybe talk to the boss for me, Mr Benjamin? I really do like it here.'

Dink hadn't seemed to notice that Trout was gathering his own goods, packing his war bag, throwing his shaving gear together, fashioning his bed-roll. Ben Trout paused and looked directly at Dink. 'I can't help you, son. I'm sorry.'

'But where am I supposed to go? What am I supposed to do now? The bewildered Eddie Guest seemed suddenly to become aware that Trout was fixing his traveling gear.

'Where are you off to, Mr Benjamin?'

'I don't know. I can't say.'

'But . . . you're boss here, Mr Benjamin!'

'No more,' Trout said, shouldering his gear. 'I'm afraid I'm as footloose as you are. 'I've been fired, too, after a mere twenty years on the job. I don't know why; but it's so. I'm pulling my freight too, Dink.'

'But why?'

'I've quit asking myself that. The man owns the ranch. He can hire and fire as he sees fit.'

'It's not fair!'

'Maybe not, but it's the way things are, and so I'm drifting. Let me by, will you?'

Dink stepped aside for Trout, speechless. Then, suddenly the kid cried out, 'Mr Benjamin, can you wait a few minutes? I'd like to go along with you if you'll have me.'

'Makes me no never mind,' Trout answered. 'But I have no idea where I'm going.'

'Neither do I, but it would make me feel a whole lot better going there with a man like you.'

Trout considered for a minute. What did it matter to him? 'I'll be waiting in the barn, Dink.'

It was a silent, melancholy duo that rode out of the K/K later that morning. Sunrise was a watery orange glow at their backs; the long, dusty West Texas plains spread out before them.

'Well,' Dink said after the first mile had passed under their horses' hoofs, unable to hold his silence, 'where are we heading, Mr Benjamin?'

'I thought I told you. I haven't an idea in the world. My only thought is to make the tanks at Alamosa tonight so we'll have water for tomorrow's travels. After that I'm not real familiar with the lay of the land.'

Dink, who had placed all his trust in the older, wiser man he believed Ben Trout to be, now appeared dismayed, as if he would melt under the high sun and puddle away in the saddle.

Trout, who had not asked for nor expected the kid's company, nevertheless decided to shine some mercy on the bleak outlook of Eddie Guest's world. Hell, he had been seventeen once, although it was hard to remember. And alone in the cold world – it had been no fun, he could remember that. Sleeping out, scrounging for any kind of meal with Indians wanting his scalp; Kiowas, mostly. All those dreary years ago. The K/K had been more than a refuge to Trout, more than a place to work. It was nearly the only home he had ever had. Did not Dink feel the same about the ranch, now lost to him?

'I've got some friends out in Arizona Territory,' Trout said, riding side by side with Dink as they traversed the long plains. 'Brothers named Wright. They inherited a few dollars and quit the K/K to go out there and start a freighting business. I got a letter from them about a year ago, asking me to come and join them. I never considered it before; now I am.'

'Tucson! That's one long way, Mr Benjamin.'

'It is,' Ben Trout agreed. 'But we're closer now than we were when we started. I figure to aim toward El Paso, rest up there for a while and then go on into the Territories.'

Dink said nothing, trying to assimilate this information. He supposed it didn't matter much just then. They still had five hundred miles of Texas land to travel over before they reached El Paso. They would be long on the trail, but at least there was a plan of some kind to cling to.

'We'll be all right,' Trout said, warming slightly to his position as mentor and guide. 'I've been saving some of my pay packet for nearly twenty years. I've no small fortune, but enough to serve me for a while in my poke.'

'I was only on the job for four months,' the

young man on the dun pony muttered. 'Can't save much over that length of time. I think I have seven dollars and a nickel or two.'

'Don't worry about it,' Benjamin Trout said. 'We're saddle partners now.'

And they were, although he hadn't planned it that way. Two cowhands reduced to riding the line. One because he was too much under thirty, the other because he was too many years over it. It stank, but that was the way of the world, Ben knew. Because he had to, he began to think of his new life as a freight line driver, of meeting his old friends the Wrights again, maybe being introduced to new friends, and who knew, some level-headed widow lady.

You could know nothing of the world until you stepped out in it, he had told himself twenty years before, broke and dispirited. Maybe, despite the circumstances, it had been time to step out again, even if it was under force. That was the thing about life: it was unpredictable.

Trout lifted the head of his sorrel pony and let it stretch out its legs in a trot for the next mile. Dink was smiling now, urging his dun pony into a run. They were heading somewhere now, and more quickly, more eagerly. That was enough.

The land was a long, lonesome series of brushy hummocks and dry swales. No water ran in the depressions, no grass grew on the hills. It seemed that Trout's idea that they had to reach the Alamosa Tanks for water that evening was correct. They were still a long way from them, and they were not carrying enough water in their canteens to satisfy either themselves or the horses for long.

The sun rose higher and became fiercer on their backs as they crossed the long, barren miles. Twenty years in this country had left Ben Trout with only a sparse knowledge of the land this far west. Dink had never traveled this way before.

'My horse isn't used to this rough use,' Dink said in a miserable voice which indicated that he was not either.

Nor was Benjamin Trout. He had gotten spoiled. There was a reason Ed Kramer had never sought to expand the K/K ranch beyond the Tascosa Valley area. In Tascosa they had water, cottonwood trees along the creeks, good grass growing most of the year. There was little of value to be had farther west.

'I ain't seen so much as a coyote,' Dink said as Ben sided him on the empty land. 'Not so much as a sidewinder in ten miles. The only thing this country has over Hades is that it's above ground.'

Benjamin Trout nodded without answering. His mouth was too dry for speaking. The kid was right. They had seen no antelope, deer or even a jackrabbit. They were carrying little food and not enough water. Sun-stunned, they rode on toward the western lands where the now-almost-mythical Alamosa Tanks stood.

There was no help anywhere nearer, no hope of civilization. They had seen few other living things, and these were only swarming gnats and the occasional high-soaring black buzzard. It was a land utterly devoid of life.

Or so it seemed until they crested the next gravel-strewn ridge, and looking down into the sandy wash below, they saw the disabled wagon tended by two hectic-looking travelers in skirts.

TWO

Halted beside Trout on his dun horse, Dink muttered through dry, swollen lips, 'I must be seeing one of those mirages you hear about.'

'If you are, I'm seeing the same one, and one of the women in it is waving to us.'

They could both see a handsome woman, her green skirt tucked up in her waistband, and a younger girl, probably her daughter, trying to right a wagon which had failed on them. Even from that distance Trout could see that the spokes on the wheel had broken from jouncing over rough country, split and landed the wagon flat on its rear axle.

The women had been going about it right. They had collected stones and carried a levering bar with them. They also, fortunately, had a spare wheel to replace the broken one. The trouble was that the rocks they had gathered to use as they jacked the wagon up were too small and probably they didn't have the pure heft to lift the wagon with the lever.

'What are we going to do?' Dink asked.

'What folks do when somebody's in trouble,' Benjamin Trout answered. 'Give them a hand if we can.'

The older woman who had been waving to them met them as they dismounted from their horses at the wagon. She wore a grateful but concerned smile which Trout understood. Who were these men appearing off the plains?

'Hello,' she said. She seemed to be a notch on the far side of thirty years old, with a trim figure and finely etched features. Her blonde hair was wind-frazzled.

'Got a little trouble, I see,' Trout said.

'Yes. I know all about how to replace a broken wheel. In theory.'

'Theory is a good thing to have, but sometimes can be mighty hard to work with,' Trout answered.

'Can you help us?' she asked eagerly.

'I think so. Dink, why don't you work your way along the wash and find us a dozen or so head-sized rocks. Not round ones, though.'

'Sure,' Dink replied. He was trying to squeeze one last drop of water from his canteen.

The woman spoke up. 'Are you boys short on water? We've got a couple of barrels full on board. Help yourselves.'

'Grateful, ma'am,' Ben Trout said. 'We were hoping to make the tanks at Alamosa tonight, but it looks like we may come up a little short.'

'I'll say you will,' the woman said with a faint laugh. 'Those tanks – if there's any water in them this time of year – are another thirty miles ahead, and those are hard miles.' She stopped. 'You two aren't army deserters or some such, are you?'

'No, ma'am. We were ranch hands until this morning. Now we're just drifters, I suppose.'

She looked at Trout's face carefully and nodded. 'Let's get on with this, shall we? By the way, my name is Beth Robinson. That over there,' she said, nodding toward the teenage girl who stood watching, hands folded in front of her, 'is my daughter, Minna.'

'Benjamin Trout,' Trout said with a nod. 'My friend's name is Eddie Guest.'

'You called him "Dink",' Minna said, having come nearer.

'It's a nickname the boys at the ranch hung on him,' Ben explained. 'They're apt to do that.'

Even then Dink was struggling back out of the wash with a fair-sized yellow boulder.

'You've got a spare wheel; that's a real help.'

'Mr Robinson, my husband, was big on being prepared,' Beth Robinson said. 'He believed in the ounce of prevention. And the country's so rough around here, it was only a matter of time before something broke.'

'And it picked today,' Ben Trout said, rolling up his sleeves. 'How's the spindle, do you know?'

'It's fine; I've already checked it. All that has to be done is take the old wheel off and replace it.'

'Where are you people traveling?' Trout asked. Using the lever he had hoisted the wagon enough for Dink to lay a second layer of squarish rocks along the first. 'Should have been a mason,' Trout kidded. Dink, perspiring freely now, grinned and placed another stone down.

'We're just going home,' Beth Robinson said. A gust of hot wind rose from somewhere and swept over her, twisting her hair, pressing her skirt against her legs.

'Home?' Trout said, surprised. 'No one lives out here.'

'Oh, yes we do,' Beth told him. 'Along that road there.'

Ben Trout had to strain to see what she was pointing out, but finally he was able to make out a twin pair of ruts scoured into the rough earth leading off far on to the empty land.

'Out there?' he said before he could stop

18

himself. He saw Beth Robinson stiffen a little.

'It suits us,' Beth said. Dink had returned with another flat stone which Trout helped him set.

'Almost got it,' Dink said, removing his hat to wipe his brow with his scarf. Sensing some sort of underlying, unhappy current between Trout and Beth Robinson, Dink scurried away again.

'Gerald, my husband,' Beth said, as they watched Dink sliding down the bank into the gully, 'bought the place sight unseen. Eighty acres on the West Texas plains with running water on the property. It was something to dream on. We didn't know how barren and isolated eighty acres could be out here where the nearest neighbor is miles away.

'But we made do, Mr Trout. It was never easy, but we always managed somehow.'

'The way you're talking . . .' Trout asked, 'is Mr Robinson gone now?'

'Two years ago this May,' she answered after a minute.

'Sorry,' Trout said in a mumble men save for such occasions. Then his voice rose. 'All right, Dink. Let's get these ladies back on the road!'

Using a large leftover boulder and the lever, Trout formed a fulcrum to lift the back of the wagon. First he wanted to know, 'Can you get the broken wheel off, Beth?'

'I have the right wrench. I don't know if I can put enough weight on it.'

'Well, we've got Dink with us. He can put his young muscle to work.' Dink looked somewhat doubtful, but proud. The younger woman, Minna Robinson, looked at Dink with admiring eyes.

'Let's go,' Trout said. 'Don't leave me holding the fulcrum for longer than necessary once we get the wagon up.'

It was a project which took more time in the planning than in the actual execution. The lug nut on the wounded wheel was cracked – that did require Dink's muscle and Ben Trout hoisted the wagon and held it while the new wheel was placed on the spindle and bolted on. In five minutes the job had been done and Beth Robinson, who knew she and her daughter had been facing a terrifying night and a long walk, leaving their goods to the elements, was effusive in her praise.

'I can't thank you enough,' she repeated at least four times.

'It didn't take us long,' Trout said, the second time she thanked him. Then he quit responding. Too much gratitude always embarrassed him. 'Let's get those rocks out from in front of the wheel so these ladies can be moving on, Dink.'

That done, they helped the women up on to their wagon bench, Dink looking uncomfortable as Minna's skirt brushed against him.

Leaning forward and down on the wagon, Beth asked, 'What did you say your destination was, Mr Trout?'

'We were planning on making our next stop in El Paso,' he said, tilting back his hat to look up at the lady.

'Oh, wonderful. You'll hardly be going out of your way at all,' Beth Robinson said, glancing at Minna.

'What do you mean?' Trout said cautiously.

'That was an invitation, Mr Trout,' Beth said. 'Come to the ranch and have fried chicken dinner with us. We've the creek running with water for your horses. All of you will feel better for being fed and watered before you travel on.'

'They say Alamosa Tanks are still a long way off,' Dink spoke up. 'We might not even make it tonight. We're not carrying much food, Mr Benjamin.' It might have been the mention of a chicken dinner that had Dink's eyes so bright, but now and then Dink would shoot a hardly secretive glance in the direction of Minna Robinson, Trout noticed.

'I don't suppose we'd be losing much time,' Trout said finally. 'There's a chance the tanks are dry. . . . All right, we'd be obliged to accept dinner from you, Mrs Robinson.'

21

'It's hardly a gift, Mr Trout. You boys got us out of a dire situation. Grab your ponies, boys – we're going home!'

The woman started the two-horse team along the little-traveled way, leaving Trout and Dink in their dust. Minna leaned far out of her seat to look back at them, her curls flying.

'Well,' Dink said, taking the reins to his horse, 'let's get going, Mr Benjamin. What are you waiting for?'

'I don't know,' Trout said honestly, as he watched the wagon gradually recede into the distance. 'Didn't the lady seem just a little too eager to you?'

'Eager?' Dink looked puzzled. 'Too eager to cook a good dinner for us to thank us for helping them, to offer us water for our horses? What's wrong with that, Mr Benjamin?'

'I don't know. Nothing, I suppose.' Dink had swung into leather; Ben still hesitated. 'I guess it's just that I don't like having my plans changed in mid-stride.'

'Your plan was pretty flat anyway, wasn't it? Mrs Robinson said the Alamosa Tanks were thirty miles farther on, and she ought to know, living out here. And if we're heading on toward El Paso, going this way is pretty much in a straight line as near as I can figure.'

'You're right,' Trout said, finally mounting his sorrel.

'You can't say we can't use the water and a dinner.'

'No,' Trout said. He still hadn't started his horse. He sat with his hands crossed on the pommel, still looking after the diminishing wagon. 'Are you sure that's why you want to go along, Dink? For a chicken dinner?'

'Why, what do you mean, Mr Benjamin? Why else?'

'Minna,' Trout said and Dink blushed to the roots of his hair.

'Ah, she's just a girl,' Dink said sullenly.

'And when's the last time you talked to one?'

'Maybe I do want to talk to her! What's wrong with that?' Trout had started his horse forward. Dink rode in silence at his side for half a mile before saying, 'Are you sure there's not another reason you are against this ride, Mr Benjamin?'

'What would that be, Dink?'

'I don't know – but if I was a man of your age, I don't suppose I'd find the Widow Robinson unappealing.'

The two men glanced at one another as they continued on across the yellow grassland. Benjamin's jaw was set, his eyes narrowed; Dink was smiling happily.

The horses' hoofs kicked up white dust as they trailed across the featureless land toward the distant horizon. 'I still don't see a building,' Dink said, wiping his forehead. Did Mrs Robinson tell you how far their ranch was?'

'No, but it sure is a far piece from where they were coming from.'

'I wonder where that was,' Dink said.

'The wagon was filled with supplies. They must have been from the trading post down at Hinkley's Ridge. You know where that is, don't you?'

'Only heard of it. Someone said it was ten miles south of the K/K.'

'If not more. A mighty long way to have to go for a sack of flour.'

Half an hour on they still did not see any ranch structures, nor the glint of the sun off the water which was supposed to flow on the Robinson Ranch. They did pass four mixed-breed cattle standing in a group around a patch of greenish graze – the only new grass they had seen so far.

The cattle had slat sides and looked miserable with their lot in life. Round brown eyes watched their passing without concern and with little interest. Trout wondered if they should not be moved toward water, but it was none of his business. He did notice they were branded cattle, as did Dink.

The brand was a standing R with a U with irregular arms. 'Gerald Robinson had a sense of humor,' Trout said with a smile.

'What do you mean?'

'He chose the brand for whoever sold him the ranch.' Dink still didn't get it, so Trout correctly interpreted the brand for him: 'Are you crooked?'

Dink smiled faintly. He was more concerned with keeping up with the wagon, with feasting on a fried chicken dinner and talking some more to Minna Robinson, maybe even walking out with her in the evening. Trout, who had seen many of these cases, saw all the signs in the young man's expression. Oh, well, Dink's plan could cause him no problems, he decided. Or could it?

Rounding a low, brushy knoll now they saw ahead a stand of four scraggly, undernourished cottonwood trees and a small house which could have had no more than four or five rooms. The RU Crooked Ranch.

The women still sat on the wagon bench, resting before they clambered down to unload the wagon. It was a little cooler, the sun lowering itself toward the far hills. There was a faint breeze and Benjamin Trout could sense water on it. The creek, whatever it was worth, was nearby. Their ponies could use it, certainly. It had been a long, dusty trail that day.

And they could use the promised chicken dinner. Minna Robinson sat smiling in the direction of Dink as he swung down from the saddle. Beth Robinson looked all business. The question was – what sort of business did the woman have in mind?

THREE

They managed to get the wagon unloaded. Sacks of flour, beans, cornmeal, a side of bacon and a peck of potatoes among assorted tinned goods and a few womanly things Trout could not identify and tried not to look at.

With that done and the women in the kitchen putting their goods away and chattering happily, Trout and Dink led their horses to water. The little silver rill trickled prettily across the sparse grassland and the high, thin clouds were dusted with gold and stained a wispy pink.

Trout watched his horse drinking, but his thoughts were elsewhere. 'Dink, let's take a walk.' Dink, crouched beside his horse, looked up with surprise.

'Where would we want to walk to?'

'There's something not quite right about the

way this river runs. You can see in the higher country that it flows a lot wider.'

'What are you thinking?'

'I just want to see what the problem is. There should be enough water flowing across the RU to spread and water a lot more grass than they have; instead it's being choked off somewhere.'

'Diverted, you mean?'

'That's what I mean. Not by a neighboring ranch, since as you can see there is none, but by a rock fall or landslide, something like that.'

And after half an hour's walk, that was exactly what they found. The face of a bluff had folded in on itself and choked off the natural course of the creek through the RU, sending a useless fork of water to the west where it died in the desert.

Crouching beside Trout on the twilit ridge, Dink commented thoughtfully, 'That could be dug out. It would give those ladies twice the water they have now.'

'It would be about a week's pick-and-shovel work for two men,' Trout observed. 'All we can do is tell them about it if they don't already know.'

'Maybe they can find a couple of men and hire them,' Dink said doubtfully. Rising he looked below them. 'That would be a pretty little grassy valley if they had enough water flowing.'

'It would be that,' Trout said. He had already

started off, striding toward the spot where they had left their horses. They could see smoke rising from the house's iron pipe chimney and Dink swore that he could smell chicken frying even at that distance.

'You've got too much imagination,' Trout said at Dink's remark.

'It comes with being young, I guess,' Dink answered. 'You know, Mr Benjamin I. . . .'

'No,' Trout said flatly. 'I know exactly what you are going to propose, and the answer's no. It's too much of a favor to ask, and I have to be traveling west to Tucson, not practicing my pick-and-shovel work.'

'What's the hurry?' Dink asked out of the near-darkness. 'You haven't even seen the Wright brothers for years. It's not like they're sitting around waiting for you.'

'No,' Trout said again just as firmly. 'Besides, no one's asked us to do the job.'

'But if they did. . . . We'd have meals for a week, help them at the same time. . . .' Dink's voice faded as they gathered up their ponies. It was obvious that he was disappointed in the older man. Ben Trout trudged on wordlessly, leading his sorrel horse.

They had taken the time to rinse off at the creek and wipe their hair back and so they were not

29

totally unpresentable at the supper table despite their dusty clothes. The women were a wonder.

Beth Robinson, her hair brushed back and pinned, wore a dark skirt and a ruffled white blouse with a cameo on a velvet choker around her throat. Minna looked as if she had just emerged from a perfumed bath somewhere; her pink cheeks and bright smile would be the envy of any town girl. She swished about the room in her pale-blue dress serving while Dink tried to avoid staring at her.

Women were a constant amazement to Ben Trout. How had they found the time to fix themselves up at the same time as they worked away in a hot kitchen preparing chicken, biscuits and mashed potatoes? Both the front and rear doors to the small house stood open now, catching the sundown breeze which had begun to cool it off.

As they ate, Ben Trout, at a non-verbal nudge from Dink, mentioned what they had found along the creek to Beth.

'Yes, I've suspected something like that for a long time. Up until last year we had a nicely flowing river. Now. . . .' She shook her head as if the battle was becoming too much for her.

'We only had two steers to take to Hinkley's Ridge to sell this time,' Minna said, hovering around Dink with a plate filled with hot biscuits.

'Ones decent enough to sell, that is.'

'You drove two cattle that far?' Dirk said in disbelief.

'Yes, sir,' Minna told him. 'Tied them beyond the wagon and took them for a stroll.'

'Amazing,' Dink said, accepting two more buttered rolls from Minna.

'Well,' Beth Robinson told the men, 'Gerald, my husband, didn't have much to leave us. He had hoped that a ranch in the West would set us up nicely. We all have our dreams. . . .' Her words trailed off. 'The RU Crooked,' she went on, using the ranch's full name, 'wasn't anywhere close to what the realtor had promised, either in his brochures or in person. But here we were and the money had been spent, so we labored on as best we could.' She paused and then mused. 'I think that trying so hard is what killed Gerald in the end. So the few cattle we're running are nearly all we have outside of the gold.'

Gold? Trout's head came up from his plate. Beth Robinson, seeing his reaction, laughed.

'I'm sorry, Mr Benjamin, but that's the reaction people always have when they hear that word. In our case we have been able to pan a little dust now and then down along the creek. I don't think we've ever gathered more than twenty-five dollars' worth at a time. Still, it's been enough to help supply us with some provisions and a few small luxuries.'

'And that was hard come by,' Minna said. Trout had a vision of the women, skirts tucked up, wading in the cold water trying to pan a little color out of the shallow creek.

'But you survive,' Ben Trout said, folding his napkin and placing it on the table.

'We do survive. Of course I don't know what I'll do when Minna leaves home—'

'—I'll never leave you, Mother!' Minna protested.

'Of course you will,' Beth said. 'The time just hasn't come yet. You'll have to leave here or marry some big lummox with half a brain and bring him out here to live.'

'Mother. . . .' Minna moaned. Trout noticed that Dink was blushing again.

It did not sound like a good set-up to Trout, the more he listened. The ranch needed more care than the women could afford. A couple of hands might be able to whip the RU into shape. Then again, to take a job way out here on a broken-down patch of earth and work it for no pay, the man would indeed have to be a lummox with half a brain. Trout glanced at Dink, who did not seem to have the same view of things. But then, Dink was looking for a home and a family like he believed he had had on the K/K. Trout was looking for a reliable opportunity to see him through his later years.

'That gold!' Minna Robinson said laughing as she finally sat at the table with them. She clasped her hands, rested her elbows on the table and smiled at each of them in turn. 'The time we did take twenty-five dollars' worth of dust into Hinkley's Ridge to purchase some supplies! Before we left town there was a rumor that there was a gold strike out our way, on a ranch that was just run by two little women. No one ever followed us, but for a while. . . .'

'For a while,' Beth put in, 'we were hoping that someone would so that we could put him to work.' She was silent for a time, looking with fond eyes at her daughter, who had already suffered much, Trout guessed.

'That's the trouble with these shoestring operations – they're born with such hopeful anticipation, but time wears them down until the wind, the cold, the loneliness just blows them and their dreams away to wait for the next hopeful, wide-eyed settler to be hoaxed into buying it.'

There was no humor in the woman's eyes now, and seemingly no hope. She rose abruptly from the table and stalked out of the room.

The young people rose and left the table as well, leaving Ben Trout to finish his coffee. The woman had herself a right little mess on the RU; that was so. In the morning Beth Robinson's troubles would mean nothing to Ben. He would be riding west, sorry for Beth Robinson and her daughter, but having no help to offer. She would have to succeed or fail on her own as all of these small ranchers did.

A faint click in the living room was followed by the rustling of garments. Trout's head turned that way. The lantern, too, had been doused in that room where he had seen Dink and Minna go. He sighed. It was none of his business what the two young people were up to, except that he was the one who had brought Dink to the RU. Pushing away from the table he rose and went that way.

What he saw was that the front door had been latched, the lantern extinguished, and Dink and Minna were crouched in front of the window. Dink had his pistol in his hand.

'Get down,' Dink hissed at Trout.

'What's happening?'

'There's someone prowling around,' Dink said.

'I saw him too,' Minna told him, keeping her grip on Dink's arm.

'Could be anybody,' Trout said, lowering himself beside the other window.

'That's just it – it could be anybody.'

'Nobody, I mean *nobody*, ever comes by way out

here,' Minna whispered with excitement.

'Probably just a wanderer looking for water or a handout,' Ben Trout said. But he, too, had drawn his pistol and was searching the darkness with his eyes. He thought he saw some movement among the cottonwood trees caught by the starlight.

'Or looking for gold,' Minna said imaginatively.

'A place to sleep.'

'Women,' Dirk said anxiously.

'Or fresh horses,' Trout added.

'Anyway,' Minna said in a rapid whisper, 'a man who meant no harm would have hallooed the house, wouldn't he? Come up to the door and knocked?'

'Yes, you're right,' Ben Trout allowed. 'We'd better find out just who this is.'

They heard then a board on the swayed porch creak as it received some weight, and the soft, nearly silent sound of boot leather sliding stealthily over wooden planks. It was unsettling behavior for a visitor unless he thought the house was unoccupied, but their horses and the smoke from the chimney made that conclusion untenable.

Whoever the stranger was, he was not behaving naturally.

There was a sudden thud, a clang, a howl of pain which broke off even as it rose from someone's throat. And a pounding on the door.

'Let me in, somebody!' Beth Robinson's voice sounded.

Minna rushed that way, her eyes wide and frightened and flung open the heavy front door to the ranch house. Beth was not alone, nor was she unarmed. The door opened to allow a square-jawed man with a month's worth of whiskers to topple in to lie against the floor. Beth came after him, a heavy cast-iron skillet in her hand.

'That'll teach a body to come sneaking around,' Beth said, hugging her daughter tightly. The man on the floor was still out cold.

'You don't know this man?' Trout asked as he slipped the side arm from the man's holster.

'I never saw him; never care to again,' Beth said, walking to the kitchen where she put the heavy skillet back on the stove. 'I went out the back door when I heard you all talking. He's alone, that's all I can tell you. I looked around.'

'I think I know who he is,' Minna said, now standing close enough to Dink so that he could slip his arm around her waist. 'I saw a Wanted poster on an outlaw named Hiram Walsh in Hinkley's Ridge today. This man looks quite like the drawing on the poster, except he has a lot more whiskers.'

'You have a good imagination, Minna,' her mother told her.

36

'I don't think so, this time,' Trout, who had been going through the man's pockets, said. In his vest pocket, the man had been carrying a much-folded Wanted poster for Hiram Walsh. Trout handed it to Beth.

Beth examined the poster carefully, then crouched down beside the unconscious man, comparing the line drawing with his face. 'I'll be . . . I think it is him,' she said, handing the poster back to Trout, who let Dink examine it across his shoulder.

'Momma,' Minna said. 'It says here they're offering five hundred dollars for his capture.'

'I know, dear, but. . . .' Beth wiped back her hair and then stopped, her actions frozen by the realization of what she had done.

'You did capture him, Momma. You surely did.'

Walsh had begun to stir and Beth walked to a cupboard and returned with a ball of twine which she gave to Ben Trout.

'Five hundred dollars,' Beth said, seating herself on the sofa. 'Do you know what that much money would mean to us, what we could do?' Minna sat beside her, eyes glowing with anticipation. Trout continued to bind the outlaw's wrists, using figure-eight knots. Then he dragged him to the wall and propped him up there.

'It's just a matter of getting him into custody,'

Dink commented. 'Where would that have to be? Hinkley's Ridge?'

'There's no jail, no law at Hinkley's Ridge. I can tell you've never been there. There's nothing there but a trading post and a saloon. No, it would have to be Riverton. If you started early in the morning, you'd be able to make it back by supper time.'

Beth's eyes were on Benjamin Trout and Dink. The look in them started out as a kind of command and then softened to a pleading expression.

Dink shrugged. 'Well, I've never seen Riverton.'

Ben Trout snapped, 'And you're never going to! We're headed for El Paso, in case you've forgotten.'

Minna looked at Dink with damp eyes. Beth continued to gaze at Ben Trout. The outlaw, Hiram Walsh, muttered a single cuss word and fell over on to his face again.

FOUR

Morning was bright. The morning birds had taken to wing. A flock of speckled brown chickens scratched at the dry earth in front of the house. The air was cool with a slight breeze rustling through the cottonwood trees. The men had been fed. It was a pretty morning – and Benjamin Trout was in a foul mood.

Well, he reflected, he had every right to be. The situation had been discussed and decided over his objections the night before. He and Dink were to take the outlaw, Hiram Walsh, to Riverton and deliver him to the county sheriff. The matter seemed almost to have been decided before Trout could voice his complaints.

He and Dink did not work for the RU Ranch; he was not heading in the direction of Riverton. It was plain none of his business. That should have been obvious to all of them, but was not.

'We can't send two women off with a known killer on such a long ride,' Dink, who seemed to have shifted loyalties, said. 'Who would watch the ranch while they were gone? Walsh might have friends in the area.'

'Who's going to watch the ranch if we do go?' Ben asked in a low growl.

Beth Robinson had an answer for that. 'I assume you know what this is, Mr Benjamin,' she said, bringing a long-barreled weapon from the closet to show him.

'Yes, I do, ma'am. It's a .50 caliber Sharps buffalo rifle. It'll take down a bull bison at 200 yards as it was designed to do.'

'Exactly,' Beth said, putting the old rifle away as if she had made her point. 'The next prowler I see around won't get a frying pan, he'll get a sample from the barrel of the buffalo gun.'

'With that five hundred dollars,' Dink put in, 'they could hire a couple of men to clean out the river bed. That would allow much more water to flow across the basin.'

'Yes,' Beth added, 'and we could also pay somebody to collect the stray cattle and drift them over closer to water. It wouldn't take a few good men more than a day or two to gather our strays and push them back toward better graze.'

'If they take the wagon,' Minna said to her mother, 'they could also bring back a few extra things we couldn't afford to get over at Hinkley's Ridge – Riverton is a bigger town by far. I'll make up a list!' Minna bounced up to do just that.

'They could even lead three or four cows and a bull back!' Beth said, catching the excitement. 'That shouldn't be too many to manage. By next spring we could have some new young blood on our range.'

Dink caught Trout's sour expression, sat on the sofa beside him and said in a low, reasonable voice, 'What's two days to us, Mr Benjamin? We could pick up some trail supplies for ourselves in Riverton – you know we're awful short. And we'd be helping two nice ladies save their ranch.'

Beth, who had overheard, put in, 'This man, Walsh, has to be put away where he can cause no more problems for society. It's our civic duty to see that he's delivered to the authorities.'

She gestured toward Hiram Walsh, who sat on the floor in the corner, his eyes blazing at times and at others clouding over with dull pain. His head was probably still ringing. He did speak once, asking, 'Don't one of you fine citizens have a dram of whiskey for a bad-hurt man?'

No one answered him; no one paid the bound outlaw a bit of attention. He might as well have not

41

existed except as a piece of their plan.

As the night wore on and the others continued to talk, Benjamin Trout felt that he had as much existence as the outlaw – no one listened to a word of his arguments.

'Aw, Mr Benjamin, don't look so gloomy,' Dink said on that new morning. 'We're going a few days out of our way to be Good Samaritans. What's two days out of your life?'

'I don't like the way it's shaping up,' Ben answered, still glowering as they trudged toward the leaning gray barn where their horses were stabled. 'I have a feeling that the women are expecting more of us. Don't forget, Dink, I have a place to go, people to see.'

'If the Wrights even remember you or recall the invitation,' Dink said a little sharply.

'These men were good friends of mine,' Ben said defensively as he snatched up his saddle and threw it over the sorrel's back. 'They won't have forgotten their offer.' Correctly reading Dink's mood he paused and said seriously: 'Eddie, we were traveling together only because you did not know where else to go. If you think this might be a place you wish to light, do as you wish. As for me, I'm delivering that bad man to the law, seeing if we can hire a couple of men willing to work out here for a few days, trying to find four or five young cattle to bring along with us when we come back, and then I'm leaving. I have my future to think about and it doesn't involve shoestringing it on some dying ranch. There's better work to be had out there. When we finish what you've obliged us to do, I'm leaving for Tucson. You can do whatever you want.'

'You're right, Mr Benjamin. The same situation doesn't fit every man. I know this whole thing just kind of popped up on you. But what some might see as a roadblock, others might see as an opportunity. I may be traveling on with you, but right now I couldn't swear to it.'

No. Trout could understand that. Eddie Guest was a young man who had had his first introduction to romance. He had never wished to leave his home on the K/K in the first place, and now he thought he had found another home with two likeable women.

Dink could see the RU improving, growing until it was something rich and fertile. Ben Trout could only think of the situation the women might find themselves in when those five hundred providential dollars were gone – and they soon would be – and they were still stuck out here in this virtual wasteland, growing older.

For Ben Trout it was no choice. He wanted a

steady job in a growing town and enough comfort to make his exit from this world as pleasant as possible.

Beth and Minna were both standing on the porch of the tiny house when they started the two-horse team out of the yard, Dink driving, his dun pony tied on behind, Trout straddling his sorrel. Hiram Walsh rode unhappily in the bed of the wagon, trussed like a captured boar hog.

Dink was looking back, and Trout glanced that way as well, knowing what he would see – Minna was waving a handkerchief enthusiastically, practically bouncing up and down. Dink lifted a hand to wave back.

What Trout had not expected to see and caught only briefly before the lady turned back toward the house was Beth's expression of hopefulness, and could it have been . . . fondness, which she allowed to linger ever-so-briefly on Benjamin Trout.

Trout shook his head. He had been without a woman for too long, and even as he frequently scolded Dink for his imagination, a stroke of the same emotion had gotten to him, it seemed.

Trout pulled the rough map Beth had sketched for them from his vest and pointed the way to Dink without saying anything.

Hiram Walsh had his own comment to put in. 'You can shorten the trip a mile or so if you take the Tehachapi cut-off.'

'You'll understand that we can't take any advice from you,' Ben Trout replied.

'Yeah, I do, but I'd like to make this ride as brief as possible. We're going the long way, this wagon bed is hard, and my head still hurts.'

'Sorry about all that, but a skillet is still better than a bullet.'

'Think so, do you? I've been shot more than once in my travels, friend, but that woman wields a wicked skillet.'

Drifting away from the wagon, so as not to hear any more of the outlaw's complaints, Ben followed the ranch wagon up the rocky trail into the low hills beyond. There the country was rife with purple sage and dotted with live oak trees. It was apparently waterless, but there were tracks of deer everywhere and cottontail rabbits scurried away from their horses' approaching hoofs. The sky held mostly clear although a few pennants of thin white clouds stretched out toward them from the far hills. The increased elevation did nothing to diminish the heat of the day. Trout dabbed at his eyes with his kerchief, keeping a watch on the country around and behind them. Dink had made one point – there was no way of knowing if Hiram Walsh had been riding alone, and the outlaw sure wasn't going to tell them the truth about that. It would be short work for a band of four or five men to take Walsh from them here in open country.

It was early afternoon with the sun still gliding high that they topped out a rocky ridge and, looking below them saw a small town spread out along the banks of a glittering river course.

'That must be it,' a weary Dink said, almost panting the words out.

'Has to be,' Ben said.

'Quit jabbering about it,' a red-faced Hiram Walsh hollered from the wagon bed, 'and get me down there. Any jail has to better than this!'

Ben Trout started to smile, found he did not have the strength. He nodded to Dink and they began making their slow, zigzag way down the trail leading to Riverton.

The county sheriff's office was not difficult to find. It was one of only two or three painted buildings along the dusty main street of Riverton. The rest had already faded to the familiar weather-grayed color of a place that was not long for this earth.

The sheriff was in. A man of thirty or so, already turning to fat, he had small dark eyes that seemed to accuse everybody. The sign on his office door said his name was Charles Earl Stout. Charlie Stout looked up at the men escorting the prisoner into his office as if they were offending him somehow.

'What's this?' Sheriff Stout demanded, looking up at the two rough men who had entered his office, escorting the hard-looking, somehow familiar, bound man.

'This,' Ben Trout said, 'is a man you might recognize. His name is Hiram Walsh. There's paper out on him and we've come to claim the reward in the name of the woman who nabbed him, Beth Robinson.'

'Hold on a minute,' Stout said, lifting a hand, still not rising to his feet. 'This is a little too rapid for me to get a handle on. You say this is Hiram Walsh. Can you prove that?'

Trout unfolded the Wanted poster Walsh had been carrying as a souvenir and handed it to the sheriff. 'You can ask him who he is,' Trout said.

'I'm Hy Walsh – lock me up, please, Sheriff!' the outlaw begged.

'Been treating you rough, have they?'

'Rough enough,' Walsh believed.

'Well, that's what your kind deserves,' the sheriff said without sympathy. 'Now, then,' he said, tilting back in his chair and folding his hands on his belly, 'you boys say the Widow Robinson captured him. Is that the Beth Robinson who has the gold mine hidden out up north somewhere?'

'There's no gold mine,' Dink said. 'Those two women take about a teaspoon of dust out of their creek each day.'

'Is that so?' Sheriff Stout said dubiously. 'Rumor has it otherwise. What, then, was this man doing up there? What was he looking for if not gold?'

'You'd have to ask him,' Ben Trout said.

'Do you think he'd tell me anything?' the sheriff asked, drumming his thick fingers on his desk top. 'Now, you say the Widow Robinson captured this man by herself – you boys work for her, I take it?'

'That's right,' Dink said almost eagerly. He took a note from his pocket that Beth had written the night before and Trout had not seen, authorizing the sheriff to give Trout and Dink the reward money. The sheriff barely scanned it.

'How am I supposed to know that what you say is what happened?' Stout asked. 'Were there any witnesses?'

'We are the witnesses,' Trout said, his temperature starting to rise. He did not like Stout much, though maybe the man was just being cautious in his job according to his own lights, seeing that it involved money.

'Sheriff, I'm a witness!' the sullen Hiram Walsh spoke up. 'Give them the reward. The lady rattled my skull with an iron skillet. Now, can I find a peaceful place to sleep in your jail?'

Stout rose from behind his desk, his expression

still far from cheerful. 'I'll grant your wish, Walsh,' the sheriff said. 'I know a little about your work in this county; it'll be a pleasure to send you off to the penitentiary.

'You boys,' he said, as he escorted Walsh to a cell, 'it'll take maybe two or three hours to get the paperwork done and for me to get the money for you.'

'All right,' Trout said, 'I guess we can wait that long.'

'You'll have to,' Stout grunted. He was busy sawing Ben Trout's knots free from Walsh's swollen wrists. Hiram Walsh, the scourge of the West, had thrown himself on to his bunk in the jail cell and was apparently asleep before Trout and Dink left the sheriff's office.

'He was still lucky,' Dink said as they stepped outside. 'Can you imagine if Beth had had that loaded buffalo gun with her?'

'Yes, and I have the feeling she would have used it. In defense of her daughter, she would have.'

'Now what do we do?' Dink asked as they stood on the plank walk in front of the sheriff's office, watching the passing men and horses.

'You can take the wagon over to the general store and start buying everything on the list the ladies gave you – I'll cover it with my own cash until Stout comes through with the reward money.'

So saying Trout fumbled out fifty dollars of his own hard-earned, dearly saved money to give to Dink.

Dink whistled silently. 'I guess that twenty years of saving can leave a man in fair shape.'

'Fair,' Trout replied, 'but it wouldn't last me long if I had to plan to live off of it. You get a receipt from the man, Dink, because I will have repayment for that money.'

'I will do that, of course, Mr Benjamin. What are you planning on doing while I'm shopping?'

'What the lady asked. I'm going to see what sort of cattle they are holding in the local pens and what their owner is asking. Then I'll ask around and see if anyone has a bull for sale.'

'That'll be a lot for us to handle on the way back to the RU.'

'It surely will; probably too much. But after finishing our shopping chores, we'll look around for some likely men. Beth wanted us to find two pick-and-shovel men to clean out the stream bed. If we can find two likely looking types, we'll ask them if they've ever pushed cattle. In this country, they probably will have at some time or another.'

'We can hire them on to help us with the cattle drive for now and to do the clean-out work on the creek later. Same pay, and an extra day of it. Should be able to find someone willing to drive cattle for that short a trip,' Dink said. 'If not, let 'em handle the wagon, and we can do it ourselves.'

'That's my thinking,' Trout agreed. 'So, let's do our shopping, eat supper after that if we can find a decent place and then start hunting some likely looking help.'

Leaving Dink to his own devices, Trout walked out into the street, asking the first man he met where he could find the town's cow pens. A gnarled finger jabbed uptown and Trout followed the indicated direction.

Ben Trout pondered as he walked the dusty streets of Riverton. He was a long way from El Paso, a long way from Tucson, and not getting any closer. Instead he was in Riverton on a buying trip for a dry-earth widow, spending his own saved money on her behalf while he waited for some money from a sheriff of unknown character, and Dink and he tried to hire two strangers as ranch hands for the RU.

It was a situation Ben did not care for; certainly it was far away from his intended plan.

Why, then, was he doing it at all? Out of a sense of loyalty to Beth Robinson, to whom he owed none? Just because the two women were alone and needed someone to help them out? Their new-hired hands wouldn't stay around long after they had finished digging out the watercourse. Beth couldn't afford to pay them for long, not if she meant to keep the bulk of that five hundred dollars she was expecting to get. The women would find themselves right back where they had started from in no time. And if the river bluff caved in again? Ben had no idea that he was going to be able to hire qualified engineers to do the job. He would find two men with strong backs willing to work for a few days' whiskey money – it was all he could hope for.

He had already accepted as fact the notion that Dink was going to be remaining behind with the women. The kid could not see beyond those sparkling eyes of Minna Robinson. Well, that was the way of young men and of the world. But Dink was inexperienced. Could he alone help to stabilize the RU?

Ben Trout shook his head and found himself thinking of several improvements he could suggest to the women. Why? He had no time to spend on someone else's troubles.

What did he care about the fate of the RU?

He chased that thought from his mind as he approached the cattle pens south of town, but found himself still thinking of the last hopeful look Beth Robinson had given him as they left the ranch. Ben sighed loudly enough to turn the head

of a man standing by. Things seemed to be pro-
ceeding well from everyone else's perspective, but
they were not going well. Not at all.

FIVE

Ben Trout bought one Holstein, two Jersey cows
and one mixed, range-tough animal of indetermi-
nate breed. He liked the look of this last one, a
reddish beast still young, but with the look of an
animal born to the range, one which would survive
hard winters and baking hot summers and bear
fine, strong, woolly calves.

Which brought him to the last point as he
handed over much of his savings to the owner of
the cattle, and asked for a receipt. 'I'm in the
market for a bull; do you know someone who
might have one?'

'That depends. I know some people who've got
fat, sleek show bulls for sale – at a price. I also
know a man who has a wild-eyed, untamed young
bull just as full of himself as he probably is of

calves. He's a handful, but can be had cheap because there's no way he can be contained or satisfied where he is now.'

'Where would that be?' Ben asked the corncob-pipe smoking old-timer.

'Right over there in that barn,' the man told him. 'I was speaking of myself. I got a young bull, but he's hell to handle.'

'I don't mean to saddle-break him,' Ben said with a faint smile and the old man nodded.

'I'll let you have a look, then. Come along.'

The old man moved with the hobbling gait of one who had once broken a leg and had it heal improperly. Seeming to be scurrying, he covered little ground as Ben strode alongside him toward the unpainted, somewhat dilapidated barn.

'He don't have a name. You wouldn't want to use the one that I call him when he starts acting up.'

'Kind of high-spirited, is he?' Trout commented as the old man swung the barn doors open.

'Yes, he is. Folks will tell you that's what you want in a bull – and they're right. But, mister, the last two times I let that creature out of the barn he broke free and stormed through the town. I'm telling you, I'm just a little too old for bull-dogging.'

'That's why you're selling him?' asked Ben as he

strolled the dark barn beside the owner.

'That's it.' The old-timer smiled. 'That and the fact that I expect to get a good price for him.'

Ben winced a little. He was spending a lot of Beth's – his? – money, and he now had the feeling that he was in the clutches of a shrewd bargainer.

He was shown the young bull, which was placid on that morning. Still, its eyes held a gleam of devilry. Almost coal black it was, sleek and well defined. Ben looked it over as best he could without entering the pen, assuring himself that all the animal's body parts were in place and seemingly able to function. It might have been a risk, but he felt obligated to purchase the animal. That was the job he had been given, after all, and the price the owner quoted in the end was not that unreasonable.

'I'll be back after a while to collect the beeves,' Ben said. 'I do need a receipt for the bull too.' They started then toward the man's shanty office once again. Thinking ahead, Ben asked: 'I'm thinking that we'll drive the cows home, but the bull might not be so easy to handle. Do you think we should lash him to the back of a wagon and lead him?'

'I would,' the old man answered as they entered his stuffy office. 'Though he'd probably be content to follow the cows where they are going, he might get a little too eager for you and delay your trip.'

'We'll try leading him,' Ben said thoughtfully. 'That reminds me, I'd like to hire on a couple of cowhands for this little job. Do you have any idea where I might find some?'

'Mr, you couldn't have come through town without seeing the saloons.'

'I did,' Ben replied, realizing he had asked an unnecessary question.

Leaving the cattle for the time being, Ben went back uptown to find Dink. The dealer in livestock had recommended a small restaurant called 'Linda's' to him, and Ben was determined to give it a try; he was getting very hungry. Dink must also be by now.

He found Dink in the alley at the rear of the general store, the wagon bed nearly full. Ben eyed the collection of mixed goods uneasily, hoping that Dink had not gone over the allotted fifty dollars Ben had given him.

Dink was in the wagon, placing a crate of apples in a secure position. The young man was perspiring freely and must have been tired, but he greeted Ben Trout with a smile.

'Sure, show up now when I'm about done!' Dink gibed, standing to mop his face with his kerchief.

'How'd you do, money-wise?' Ben wanted to know.

'Forty-eight dollars and some change. The man's totaling the receipt for me right now.'

'Looks like enough food to feed an army through the winter,' Ben commented as Dink swung down from the wagon.

'You know how it is with food – always looks like a lot until you start in on it,' Dink said. 'And Beth's got more mouths to feed now.'

Ben didn't respond to that. He, himself, did not plan on being one of the extra mouths for long. He would deliver what they had agreed on to the RU, make sure that he was repaid for what he had personally spent and then be on his way to El Paso. Alone, the way it looked now.

Dink returned with the receipt from the store-keeper, slapped it in Ben's hand along with some change. In his hand Dink held a small bag.

'What's that?' Ben asked, nodding at the bag as he carefully folded the receipt and put it away with the others.

'This? Something the women didn't think of, but I did,' Dink said with some pride. 'Vegetable seeds. Do you like butternut squash?'

'I won't be here in the fall,' Ben said.

'I just asked. I've also got tomatoes, pole beans, cabbage, just about anything you can think of.'

'Trading in your spurs for a garden hoe, are you?' Ben said lightly.

'The earth is a bountiful provider,' Dink said, growing briefly philosophical. 'A handful of seeds can feed a family for months, years. What's the matter, Mr Benjamin, don't you like to eat?'

'I do, and that's what I intend to do now,' Ben said, swinging aboard the sorrel. He led the way toward Linda's Restaurant which he had already located on the main street, Dink following in the wagon with his dun horse tethered behind again.

'I suppose I'll have to lead the dun, or you'll lead my sorrel,' Ben told Dink as he tied up the wagon in front of the restaurant. 'We're taking along a tethered bull.'

'How big?' Dink asked. 'How old?'

'He doesn't have his size yet,' Ben told him. 'He's not yet three years old, but he's got a lot of spirit.'

'Well, I suppose between the two of us we can handle him for the four hours or so it'll take us to get him home.'

Home, he said, not 'to the RU'. Yes it was pretty obvious where Dink's head was, what he was hoping for.

They ate well if not sumptuously at Linda's Restaurant, and it was almost with shock that they emerged to find the sun still high in the sky. It seemed that they had already put in a full day's work. But they had only begun.

'Now we find some men?'

Ben nodded, 'Now we find some men to hire, but first we go back and talk to Sheriff Stout about the reward on Hiram Walsh. I haven't got enough money to carry on like this, and Beth Robinson won't have any at all to work with without that money.'

It turned out that it was not necessary to find the sheriff. Before Ben could swing into leather, the round, bustling form of Sheriff Charles Stout, sunlight glinting on his badge, could be seen approaching the restaurant.

'Are they serving those breaded pork chops with apple sauce today?' was what Stout asked Ben, at the same time handing him an official-looking manila envelope. 'I always did like those.'

'I saw them on the menu, but I didn't have them,' Ben said, opening the envelope to flip through the stack of bills it contained.

'You should have. I don't know what Linda does to them, but they're excellent. Goodbye, men; I doubt I'll be seeing you again.'

'I doubt it, too, Sheriff. Enjoy your lunch.' Ben tucked the envelope away in an inside pocket in his leather vest.

'Aren't you going to take out what you're owed?'

Dink asked.

'I mean to sit down at the table with Beth and do it together,' Benjamin Trout told his younger friend. 'That's a more respectable way to do business.'

'I can't see that it matters,' Dink said, unwrapping the reins from the brake handle, 'but seeing as you say it's so, Mr Benjamin, I'll keep that in mind for the future.'

Leaning forward on the bench seat, studying the town, Dink asked, 'Where now?'

'The nearest saloon will do,' Ben Trout said. Dink shrugged with his eyes and started the horses forward along the street.

Walking into the smoky, low-ceilinged saloon, Ben Trout knew what he was looking for: two broad-shouldered young men who had not been drinking enough to be in their cups, but had had a few to lift their spirits and make them bold enough to wish to try a new enterprise. They didn't have to be handsome, bright or especially law-abiding, just strong with young muscle and manageable for a few days.

While Dink waited outside with the wagonful of goods, Ben bought himself a mug of green beer and wandered about the room, dismissing the old and the frail-appearing, the sullen and the combative.

He thought he found his pair sitting at a corner table playing a desultory game of cards with an almost empty pitcher of beer on the table between them. Jim Hicks, although Ben had not yet learned his name, was a thick-chested, copper-haired man in his mid-twenties; his partner was Clarence 'Clare' Tillitson, who had the hands of a hard-working man and a likely grin. Ben approached them.

'You fellows cowhands?' Ben asked, perching on a nearby table.

'Have been,' Jim Hicks said, smiling pleasantly. 'At the present time, you might say we're fancy free.'

'How's your poke holding out?' Ben asked, seeing no sense in wasting time. The men could either be hired to work or they would decline and he could continue elsewhere with his search.

'You can see we're playing for matchsticks,' Clare Tillitson said, indicating the table stakes for their card game.

'Are you offering us a job?' Jim Hicks asked.

'I've got something that might appeal to you,' Ben said. 'It would only be for a few days, though.'

'What are you thinking of paying?' Clare Tillitson asked, looking at his cards, then at Ben's face again.

'Four dollars a day apiece,' Ben said. The wages

were superior for that time and place, and the two men looked at each other questioningly.

'Did you say that this was cattle work?' Jim Hicks asked, sliding back from the table a little.

'Only about four hours of it,' Ben said with his own crooked smile. Clare Tillitson was perplexed. Ben told the younger man, 'The rest is pick-and-shovel work – I don't know if you boys would be willing to go at it.'

'Dangerous, is it?' Hicks asked with a squint. That was a lot of money for common labor. 'I mean, it's not down in a mine, is it?'

'No, nothing like that. It will take me a little time to explain it, men. I'll buy you a fresh pitcher of beer if you're willing to listen. Then we'll have to be trailing out while there's sunlight.'

'Planning on traveling far?' Hicks asked.

'Just those few hours. We should make it back to the RU by sunset. Let me get you that pitcher of beer.' As he leaned forward to rise, Hicks got a glimpse of the envelope in Ben's inside pocket and the sheaf of bills it held. Ben immediately secured the envelope that Sheriff Stout had given him for Hiram Walsh's capture, but Hicks had quick eyes. Right then he had quick, greedy eyes.

He asked Clare as Ben walked toward the bar, 'Who is that guy? It seems like I've seen him somewhere.'

'Sure you have. That's Benjamin Trout of the K/K,' Clare told his partner.

'What's he doing way out here, then? And why did he say we were riding to the RU – wherever that is?'

'He must have got himself a new job he likes better.' Clare Tillitson shrugged, looking in Ben's direction.

'But he was foreman on the K/K . . . hold it a minute,' Hicks said in a low hiss, gripping his friend's forearm across the table. 'Now I remember hearing about the RU!'

'Well?' Clare prompted.

'Gold,' Hicks said, keeping his voice to a whisper. 'I heard some men saying that the RU was run by a widow woman and her daughter, and that they had a hidden gold mine out there.'

'Think it could be true?'

'Why else would the respectable foreman of a big ranch like the K/K leave? A widow lady with a gold mine could offer some inducements. Not only that,' Jim Hicks said, inching nearer, 'I got a glimpse of the wad of cash that Trout's carrying, and believe me it's fat.'

'When did you . . . how?'

'Just take my word for it,' Hicks said as Trout started back toward the table. 'Ask yourself why the RU wants to hire pick-and-shovel men. Not to push cows. There's something going on out there, Clare, and I think if we go along with it, we're set for a big payday.'

SIX

The bull was still in a placid mood when it was led from the barn and into the bright sunlight to stand and blink. Hicks and Clare each had a rope around its neck, tugging from opposite sides, and they were trying now to position the animal behind the wagon to be tethered there.

Beside the wagon Ben sat loosely in the saddle while Dink stood beside him, watching the bull be tugged slowly forward.

'Shouldn't we give them a hand?' Dink asked.

'No,' Benjamin Trout said. 'You don't hire a man to do a job and then do it for him.'

'I guess not,' Dink said uncertainly. 'I haven't had much experience at being a boss.'

'You're about to get some,' Ben told him. 'You're the boss now; I already told Hicks and Clare that.'

'Why me?' Dink asked with some uneasiness.

'Because you are the one who's going to stick around to see that they do their job. I won't be here, Dink. I'll probably spend the night at the RU, then I'm back on the trail to El Paso. I'm going to trade off with you and drive the wagon. You can lead this little drive of ours.'

Dink, looking vaguely discouraged, only nodded as the new-hires finished their job. The four heifers were then hied out of the pen by the man who had sold them to Ben, and Dink had to look to Ben for advice.

'Get them started ahead of us,' Ben advised. 'That'll keep the bull with his mind on what's ahead instead of trying to turn around to see what's behind him.'

Dink then led the way out, leading Ben's sorrel horse, the two cowboys and the heifers behind him. Ben followed in the wagon, leading the bull, which was still minding its manners. The first little stretch was four blocks through the center of town which surprised or startled no one along the way. Then it was out on to open country with Dink cutting trail for the new men to follow. Ben divided his time between watching the bull, studying the cowboys as they handled the docile heifers, and glancing at the western sky to judge how much light they had left to complete their journey.

He had hopes for a warm meal and a good night's sleep after settling the cattle and unloading the wagon. Then, come morning, he would leave the RU Crooked to the well-intentioned and wishful and proceed on his long journey west.

At one point along the way, the black bull suddenly became balky for no apparent reason and began to tug the wagon from side to side by its leads, but outside of that it gave Ben no problems en route.

With sundown casting a golden glow against the sky they came to the rise in the land which overlooked the long, dry valley below where the RU rested. Defiant little ranch that it was, there was something touching about it at this time of evening. Perhaps it was because it simply endured, still held the hopes of Beth and Minna, fragile though those might be.

Dink started the small group down the road to the RU. Ben leaned on the brake pole to slow the heavy wagon. Reaching the flat, they lined out directly toward the yard. There would be time to water the stock later. Dink obviously wanted to show the women how they had succeeded in their mission.

Home were the saviors of the ranch.

On the porch, drawn by the sounds of the cattle approaching, the whistles and shouts of the drovers, Beth and Minna stood close together watching the arrival. Ben drew up in front of the house as Dink let the cattle wander where they would. He was guessing, rightly, that they would find the creek, drink their fill and stay near it, having no idea where else to go.

'Did you get a look at the cattle?' Ben Trout called to Beth on the porch.

'Not much of one; I guess that will have to wait until morning. I see that, though!' she said, pointing at the big black bull tethered on behind. Minna moved nearer as if she would touch the bull.

'I wouldn't do that,' Ben said, swinging down. 'He's just play-acting. He's not really that calm.' Ben removed his hat, wiped his brow and placed one boot on the swaying step of the porch. 'Which brings this up, Beth: seeing that you're his owner now, do you want us to try to get him in the barn, stake him out, or just cut him free to roam?'

'What do you think is best?' she asked.

'I think we can just turn him loose. The cows are still here, and he'll find the water soon enough. Everything a healthy young bull could want.'

Ben didn't get the smile in return he was expecting from Beth Robinson. Maybe she just didn't have much of a sense of humor.

'What's his name?' Minna asked, her eyes bright

even in the dim light of dusk.

'He hasn't one – that's one thing you can take care of.' Turning back to Beth, he said, 'How about getting a lantern out here and we can take the supplies in.'

'As soon as the bull is freed.'

'As soon as the bull is freed,' Ben agreed.

'I see you brought along two men to work on the bluff wash-out,' Beth said, lifting her chin toward the creek.

'Everything you asked for, and some extra,' Ben answered.

'Extra? What?' Beth enquired.

'Vegetable seeds,' Ben muttered before walking to the rear of the wagon to untie the bull.

It took less than half an hour, with everyone working, to get the supplies tucked away in the kitchen pantry. Beth stood back, looking at her cache with pride. They now had everything they needed to last them for months.

'Let's sit down and talk business,' Ben Trout suggested, going to the small kitchen table. He placed the envelope containing the reward money on the table and withdrew his stack of receipts from his own expenditures. 'Have you got a pencil?' he asked, and Beth went to a coffee mug on the counter which held a few miscellaneous items and removed the stub of a pencil from it.

She glanced once toward the kitchen door. Dink and Minna had retreated to the front room. The last time Ben had seen Hicks and Clare they were sitting on the front porch, having a smoke.

'This doesn't have to be done right now,' Beth said, seating herself opposite Ben.

'When is a better time?' Ben asked removing his hat, running his fingers through his dark hair. 'This is all a part of the same business; let's get it finished up and then you can go about whatever it is you want to do.' He paused for a moment, smiled at the handsome woman sitting there and added, 'It will make me feel better to have it finished.' They started with the large items and worked their way through them. 'I may have spent too much for the bull,' Ben apologized.

'Was there any other choice?' Beth asked.

'Not that I know of.'

'Well, then . . . we asked you to buy a bull and you did the best you could,' Beth answered. Her attitude seemed a little free and easy to Ben.

'Beth,' he said, 'you're going to have to be very careful with the remainder of your money.'

'I realize that,' she answered a little stiffly as if she had been insulted. Ben just looked at her for a moment longer, then nodded.

When the totaling had been completed and both pronounced themselves satisfied with the final tally, Ben returned his money to his scuffed wallet and Beth slowly gathered up what was left of the reward for Hiram Walsh, tucking it away in her apron pocket.

'Don't scowl, Mr Benjamin,' she said. 'I'm going to put it away in the strongbox in my room as soon as we get up from the table.'

'Was I scowling?' Ben asked. 'I'm sorry. I didn't mean for it to seem like I was nagging you. It's just that I was. . . .' he looked down at his big, weather-beaten hands and fell silent.

'What? Worried about us, Mr Benjamin?' Beth asked. She touched his hand lightly and there was a faint, warm smile on her lips. 'It's all right to say that. I know how it is; I've been worried about us for years.'

'Things will be better now,' Ben said uncomfortably. He was wriggling emotionally. He was afraid he would say something more to Beth, and his schedule did not allow for more conversation.

'Yes,' Beth said, placing her hands on her lap. 'That brings us to another point, doesn't it? These young men you brought out here – can they be trusted?'

'I don't know. Is there something bothering you about them?'

'Not really, except the way they have been looking at Minna.'

'The town was fresh out of young men who don't like to look at girls,' Ben said, again trying for a joke. Again it fell flat; Ben had about decided that humor was not his area.

'It's the way they look, Ben, do you understand? I saw them while we were unloading the wagon. They looked at her as if she were some saloon girl. I didn't care for it at all.'

'They should only be here for a couple of days, long enough to clean out the cave-in along the bluffs.' Ben paused, smiled and told her, 'Besides, Dink will be around to keep an eye on them.'

'Eddie Guest,' Beth said, reminding herself. To Ben she said, 'I'm trying to avoid calling him by his nickname. He can't like it much.'

'He never seemed to mind back on the K/K.'

'But that was among his fellow male workers, half of whom probably had their own nicknames like Red, Whitey, Tex and Smoky. It made him feel that he was accepted among equals. He can't want me to call him Dink . . . nor Minna.'

'I suppose not,' Ben admitted.

'How old is he, Ben?'

'Dink? I think he said that he was seventeen, going on eighteen. Why?'

'It's just that he seems little more than a boy next to those two hulking men you hired.'

'Maybe. But he was doing a man's work on the

K/K,' Ben reminded her.

'Still. . . .' Beth said, looking down at the table now. It was obvious that she wanted to say something more. Finally with a sharp inhalation she lifted her eyes again to Trout and said, 'I'd feel a lot better about things, Ben, if you would stay around here just until those two are finished with their work.'

'I've got to be going on my way, Beth. You know that.'

'You said yourself that it would only take them a couple of days. Can't you wait that long?' She grew more emphatic. 'I'll pay you for it, Ben. Whatever wage you ask! Just for two days. Please. . . ? Please?'

Ben lay awake in the near silence of the desert night. Once he heard a nearby owl hoot and the howl of a far distant coyote. Beyond that there was not a sound to keep him awake. No one moved about the house. The two new hands had said they preferred to sleep outside, and it was a fine, warm night for it; besides, there was obviously no space for them in the small house. There was nothing to keep Ben Trout from sleeping; still he could not manage it.

Rolling over under his single blanket, Ben found his mind continuing to turn about matters that should not have concerned him. Who were these two young hands that he had hired so hastily? Just men, no different from the dozens of unemployed, drifting cowhands that could be found in any Western town on any day. Beth seemed to have her suspicions of them, but that might have only been her motherly protectiveness.

All the same, Eddie Guest was in charge of them now; it was none of Ben's affair. Ben had not hired on to the RU, nor had he adopted Dink. He had his own thought-out plan summoning him back to the trail west. The women were struggling and would continue to struggle. Even with Ben's help they would have a hard time of it. That was the way things were in this country.

He had done all he could for them, all there was time to do. Let the two new-hires dig out the cave-in, let Dink manage the RU as best he could. Benjamin Trout was on his way to Tucson to join the Wright brothers' freight company.

Rolling over again, he yawned and finally fell off to sleep.

Ben Trout was up with the first light he saw, which was that glinting uncertainly through a high slit window in his room. Dressing, he made his way to the kitchen where Beth bustled around the stove and Minna bustled around Dink, who looked well-satisfied with himself.

Clare Tillitson and Jim Hicks had eaten earlier, he was told, wanting to get a start on their digging while the desert was still cool.

'You laid the job out for them?' Ben asked Dink.

'I did, though anyone could see what the problem is and what has to be done.'

Ben frowned a little, realizing that he had been the last one up on that morning. It was a bad habit and one easily fallen into. Beth placed a cup of coffee on the table in front of him and surprisingly, almost casually, placed a hand on his shoulder. When he glanced up, he could see that she was smiling – tiredly, but she was smiling.

'The bull hasn't budged,' Dink told Ben. 'He's sniffing around the heifers like he's interested but doesn't know exactly what to do.'

'When it's their time, he'll know,' Ben muttered almost as if he were angry. He wasn't used to discussing such things in front of females. There was something else bothering him, and he knew it but did not want to admit it.

'Well,' Dink said, rising and dabbing at his lips with his napkin, 'I guess I'd better ride up to the gap and see how those two human dynamos are doing. There's some that only work hard when they're being watched.' He paused. 'I guess you'll be striking out before I get back, Ben. I just wanted to tell you thanks for everything.' He offered

Benjamin Trout his hand.

'Save that for a while,' Ben said with a scowl. 'Nobody around here, including the ranch manager, seems to be giving a thought to the RU's assets. I'm riding up to the eastern range to look for cattle and do a head count. If I find a few I can push toward the river without a lot of trouble, I'll bring them in.'

Dink murmured some words of thanks and Minna let out a few happy, girlish squeals. When the two youngsters had gone out of the room and left the house, Ben slammed down his empty coffee mug on the table and asked Beth Robinson in a growl:

'Are you happy now?'

'Why, Ben,' she answered, 'as long as you're happy, I'm happy.'

Then she went out the back door to do something in the yard and Benjamin Trout, still grumbling, went to saddle his sorrel horse and put in a day's work.

SEVEN

For most of the morning, Ben scoured the hills and brushy hollows, looking for strayed cattle. There were quite a few more RU branded steers than he would have imagined bunched in the small places where water seeped and grass greened the land. A gather could produce two or three dozen at a guess. And if they were driven to the flats below when the river returned to its normal course and volume, they along with the new stock might begin to thrive.

That prospect required many undertakings to bring to fruition. The cattle would have to be brought down out of the hills, of course, but first there would have to be a good source of water and graze provided. That meant, as Ben knew from long experience, the construction of feeder dams to spread the river flow out across the dry grass-lands. In his time he had done that many times, but usually with a full crew to help in the construction of the earthen dams.

Ben had seen at least two dozen cows among the wild beeves. That rogue of a black bull they had brought back to the RU should be able to make friends among them and repopulate the barren land, if he was all that Ben believed him to be.

There would be no more lashing two steers on behind the wagon and towing them to Hinkley's Ridge to sell for money to purchase a few necessities. Beth could afford to hire a crew at round-up time to drive the cattle to the best local market, whether that would be Hinkley's Ridge or Riverton. Assuming she didn't wish to spend the time on a long drive to one of the railheads.

Ben vowed to have a long talk with Dink that evening. Yes, the young man was inexperienced, but all of these operations should be within his capabilities.

Ben rode past a trio of sad-looking cows, angling upslope. The animals deserved better treatment than they had gotten since the river went nearly dry. There was a hot, dry wind gusting as Ben achieved the crest of the yellow hill. He paused, opened the front of his shirt to let the breeze dry his chest and looked down across the forlorn land.

The RU could have been something, he decided, with the proper management. Gerald Robinson had not been a cattleman, nor even a Westerner from what Beth had told them. Just another man with a dream of life in some wide open spaces. The cattle brand itself was a legacy to Robinson's own bitterness, though the land agent might not have deserved the blame he got. The land seemed to be as represented, but not necessarily as Robinson had envisioned it. Dreams and reality do not always mingle well.

Benjamin thought he would suggest to Beth Robinson that the new cattle and all future ones be branded differently. The 'R' for Robinson would stay, of course, and the 'U' if she was partial to it. But the prongs of the 'U' should be straightened out. Having the RU ranch should be a source of pride; the RU Crooked brand was a constant reminder of one man's faded dreams.

Ben shook his head. What did any of that have to do with him? He would make his few suggestions to Beth and to Dink and then continue on his way. Between them they could figure out what they wanted to do with the exhausted ranch. He nudged the sorrel a little with his boot heels and moved farther along the ridge, intending to find a spot where he could look down along the collapsed bluff and make sure the pick-and-shovel men were making progress.

They were small in the distance when Ben finally could make out Jim Hicks and Clare. At the moment no picks were flashing silver in the air. The two were taking a break, apparently. Well, they were not prisoners, were not slaves. The sun was hot, the canyon airless. They could not toil constantly.

The two were young and very strong; Ben had no doubt they would finish the job. He only hoped that it could be done in the two days that Beth had asked him to remain and keep an eye on the working men. He turned his horse away as the men again lifted their tools and returned to their work.

'What are you thinking, Jim?' Clare Tillitson asked, resting on his pick. His shoulders bulged with muscle from years of such work. Neither man had on a shirt.

'Just what I thought before,' Hicks said, shoveling some of the loosened material away. 'They're planning on doing some serious mining up here. I've had some experience, as you know. Well, the way I see it is that they need an increased flow of water to go at it.'

'How's that?' Clare asked, interested.

'There's a bit of equipment called the long-tom,

81

Clare. What it is is a kind of long sluice box for separating out the gold from the gravel, but it requires a lot of water to use. Four men usually operate one, and they can just work along it picking out gold nuggets like cherries.'

Jim Hicks wasn't finished with his specious reasoning yet. 'Look at this place. What do they need with more water – for four cows!' Hicks laughed. 'No, sir, there's gold here like everyone always said, and a lot of it if they're going to all this trouble. There's a fortune to be made here, and we are going to get our share. All we need,' Hicks said, stopping to mop his brow, 'is a little help.'

It was sundown of the following day, as Ben and Beth Robinson sat on the front porch watching the colors of the evening sky, when Dink rode his dun horse toward them, his teeth flashing a happy smile.

'Here it comes. You have to come and see it!' His horse moved in a tight circle as he called to the two people on the porch.

'Come and see what?' Beth Robinson asked, standing from her porch chair.

'The river, ma'am! It's been freed of its bonds and it's flowing like a roaring tide.'

Ben stood, looked to the west, hands on his hips, and slowly smiled. Dink was right. Even from there he could see that the river was wider, moving more swiftly. The late sun shone on its face, silvering and staining it with the colors of sundown.

'Well, I guess we owe those two pick-and-shovel men our thanks. They seem to have done their job,' Beth said.

'And caused no harm,' Ben added. It made him feel better about hiring Hicks and Clare. They had bothered no one and gone about their work in an apparently praiseworthy fashion.

'And caused no harm,' Beth agreed, feeling a little foolish about her earlier doubts. 'I think they ought to be given a bonus, Ben,' she said.

'No,' Ben Trout said. 'That's money you don't have. They were hired to do a job, and they did it. They were paid well enough.'

'All right, boss. I suppose you're right,' Beth said with just a touch of sarcasm.

Minna had come out of the house, and from horseback Dink repeated his news, and his request that they all come and witness the rapidly flowing river. Minna rushed eagerly to Dink and was swung up beside him on his dun horse. Together the two started toward the river bottom.

'Aren't we going, Ben?' Beth asked.

'I've seen rivers run before,' Ben said, not sure why his mood had turned sour.

'So have I,' Beth said from out of the shadows. The lantern inside the house caught her profile and framed it appealingly. 'But I haven't seen this one running full for a very long time. It could mean new life for the land, new life for us, Ben. A chance to again try to make something of the RU.'

She was right, of course, and the way she said that made Ben feel ashamed of his manner. The river, restored to its old course and flow, held the promise of revival for the cattle, for those who occupied the land. As Dink had wanted them to rush that way and see what was happening, Beth wished to share her joy in a successfully completed, life-bringing project.

And here was Benjamin Trout grumping around.

'We'd better have our look, I suppose,' Ben said, 'before Dink bursts.'

She took his hand gently in hers which somehow did not surprise Ben and they went from the porch to view the new marvel. 'I know,' Beth told him as they walked across the dry grass, past the cattle, 'that you have been trying to tell me that I need to be more practical about things if I'm going to make a go of it.'

'I just. . . .' Ben began, but she held up a hand.

'You have been trying to get me to watch my money, and I appreciate it. I do need reminders to keep a better watch on my affairs.' She took in a deep breath, throwing her head back. 'Mr Gerald

84

Robinson was a fine man, Ben. But he was what you might call a dreamer, giving little thought to tomorrow. I never really learned to be practical, though with a daughter and a ranch to run, you'd think that I would have.'

Ben gave her no answer. He was aware that Beth was still looking up at him. There was a question in those eyes, but he could not answer it now.

Ahead, the two young people stood near the bank of the rapidly flowing creek. Minna performed an impromptu jig, holding her skirts up while Dink just stood watching the river flow, a wide grin on his face.

'They can feel the rush of new life,' Beth said quietly.

'They're young,' Ben said, puzzling Beth, and perhaps stilling her own enthusiasm.

They watched the river stretch its limbs and take over its lost territory, shining in the late light. It was a living thing that had nearly been strangled and found its way back to life. 'It's all thanks to you, Ben,' Beth said, squeezing his hand.

'I don't know how you figure that,' Ben answered. 'You knew what had to be done, and you would have gotten it done. I'm not the one who did the digging. I'm not the one who banged Hiram Walsh's skull with a frying pan.'

'No, but you were the one who knew how to put

everything together to make it work. I can tell that you are used to managing things – that must have been what you did on the K/K Ranch, manage the business affairs.'

'Not exactly,' Ben muttered, not wishing to discuss the K/K. The wound he felt from being fired off the ranch had still not developed any scar tissue.

'Look at it!' Beth exclaimed, with a fresh burst of enthusiasm. 'Why, this week we should be able to start pushing the lost cattle down from the open range, out of the hills.'

'I'd give it a while longer to let the grass recover. You might need to haul in some hay otherwise. Whatever you and Dink decide I'm sure will be fine. You can afford some patience now.'

'Everyone but you, Ben,' Beth said. She had turned to face him. He looked over her shoulder at the river, which now was slowing its initial surging rush across the flats. Beth would not be stilled. 'Everyone but you should practice a little patience. Meantime you're continuing your mad dash across the far lands, not even knowing where you're going or what you will find when you get there.'

'It's what I've set my mind to, Beth.'

'And you're going to stick to it whether it's for the best or not.'

'I'm going to stick to it,' he said, looking into those dark eyes of hers. He might have said more, but just then two muddy, soaked sandhogs appeared out of the darkness. They had their tools in their hands; Jim Hicks had his arm thrown around Clare's shoulder. Both men were smiling.

'It busted loose faster than we expected,' Hicks told them. 'We had to do some mighty scrambling to get out of the way.'

'It doesn't look like you quite made it,' Beth said, studying their filthy, sodden clothes.

'Good enough – we didn't get washed away,' Hicks said cheerfully.

'We can wash off in the river,' Clare said. 'There's plenty of water for that. Then we were thinking of striking out for Riverton.'

'Tonight?' Minna, who had been listening, asked.

'Yeah, tonight,' Jim Hicks said. 'It's still early and we mean to celebrate a little. As soon as we. . . .'

'As soon as you get paid, yes of course,' Beth said. 'Whenever you boys are ready, just come up to the house – the back door to the kitchen – I'll have your money ready for you.'

'Thank you, ma'am,' Hicks said, nodding.

'You're welcome, boys. We'll be thanking you for a long time. The river is flowing freely again because of you.'

'We just did what we were told,' Clare said.

'You two come back and see us again sometime,' Minna said. Her eyes were on Jim Hicks. Dink, Ben noticed, had lost his smile.

'Oh, we will, you can count on that,' Hicks said.

'We surely will,' Clare Tillitson echoed.

Then the two well-muscled men strolled off toward where they had left their gear and their horses.

'Let's get up to the house if we're going to have supper tonight,' Beth said, taking Minna's hand.

Dink still stood frowning, looking after Hicks and Clare, who were chatting, laughing, no doubt discussing how they were going to spend their pay that night.

Dink turned, grabbed up the reins to his dun and started off toward the house beside Ben Trout.

'What was that all about?' Dink asked Ben, meaning the conversation that had just gone on between the women and the pick-and-shovel men.

'Just polite talk,' Ben said, without looking at Dink, 'or what passes for it.'

'I didn't like it. I didn't like the way Minna was talking to that man at all.'

'Just polite conversation,' Ben said again. 'Besides, I guess she can talk to anyone she likes. You don't have that kind of claim on her.'

'I don't have any kind of claim on her,' Dink said. 'I just didn't like it, that's all. Is that all right with you, Mr Benjamin?'

'She'll never even see the man again,' Ben said as they approached the front of the house.

'I just don't like the man, that's all,' Dink muttered, and Ben only nodded. At seventeen-almost-eighteen Dink was feeling jealousy and frustration. It couldn't be helped. Ben didn't admit it, but he was slightly troubled himself about the way the two had assured them that they would be back. It seemed that there had been the barest shadow of a threat in their words, but probably he was imagining it.

While Dink and Minna were cleaning up for dinner, Ben again seated himself at the kitchen table with Beth, waiting for Hicks and Clare to call for their pay. Beth had counted their money carefully and put it into two identical packets. To Ben she looked a little nervous.

'What's the matter, Beth?' he asked her.

'Nothing. Just me being silly again, but I'll be happier when those two have their pay and leave. I'll lock the door after they ride away. I never liked having them on the ranch, and I still don't.'

'You and Dink.'

'What?'

'Dink doesn't like having them here either,' Ben told her.

'Well, in his position I can understand that,'

Beth said with a small smile. She could hardly be unaware of Dink's infatuation with Minna. 'But I'm supposed to be a grown woman.'

'You are that,' Ben said without thinking. He had been admiring the graceful curves of her body. Beth lifted her eyes, seemed ready to snap out something and then just turned silently pink. They talked aimlessly of a few things then – Ben did bring up the subject of the RU brand which he felt diminished the ranch.

Ten minutes later Clare and Jim Hicks showed up at the back door and were given their pay. 'Well, that's that,' Beth said, turning back into the room. 'They've done their job and gone. It's all over. We've seen it through – that part of it.'

'Let's hope so,' Ben said, rising from the table. Beth looked up at him with some puzzlement.

'What do you mean, Ben?'

'Nothing.' He shrugged. 'Nothing at all. I suppose that some of your attitude and Dink's have rubbed off on me. I find that I don't trust those two either now.'

'But they're gone now, Ben. They won't be back. Why would they come out here again?'

'I don't know,' Ben said, although he had the barest glimmering of an idea why they might. 'All the same, maybe I'd better stay around a couple of more days to make sure they don't.'

Beth only nodded. Was Ben making some kind of excuse to stay around the ranch? She could have told him that he needed none. She sensed that he would not appreciate any comment she could make at that time, and remained silent as he went off to clean up for supper.

When he was gone, Beth got up again and quite deliberately locked the back door.

EIGHT

'You're crazy,' Cyrus Sullivan said, taking in both Jim Hicks and Clare Tillitson with his scathing glare. 'Do you know that? Both of you – you're crazy as loons.'

'Cyrus,' Jim Hicks said, leaning his arms on the poker table where they had gathered, 'we came to you because you're known as a man of vision. If you can't see the possibilities of this deal, maybe we should be talking to someone else.'

'Maybe you should,' Cyrus Sullivan, a hulking man with a drooping, grey-streaked red mustache told them. 'It sounds like a pipe dream to me,' he said, although avariciousness kept him from totally closing his mind to the proposition that Hicks and Clare had brought to him. Sullivan had taken a flyer on more than a few wild schemes. Some of them had made him very wealthy. Others had left him with pennies in his pockets and sawdust in his mouth. The mention of gold had perked his ears as it always did, but how was he to trust the credibility of these two young roughnecks?

Clare spoke up. 'We were out there only today finishing the run for long-tom mining,' he told Sullivan confidently.

'Yes,' Cyrus said, stretching and drawling out the word, 'and did either of you see any color?'

'No,' Hicks said with deliberate nonchalance, 'they wouldn't put us anywhere near the actual strike.'

'But you know those women have gold,' Clare put in, drinking from his beer mug. 'I mean, everyone from here to Hinkley's Ridge knows that those women do all their shopping with gold dust.'

'Yes, I've heard that,' Sullivan said, sipping from his own beer mug. 'But that doesn't mean much. You don't see a big house on that property, do you, or those women wearing finery and jewels?'

'They've just now decided, or had it suggested to them, that they open up their mining operation,' Hicks said, leaning forward across the table, careful to keep his voice down.

'By these new-hires they have on the ranch?' Sullivan asked, still meditating on the pluses and minuses of this idea.

'Sure, and where did they get the money to hire

them? Or, where did they come up with a convincing idea for them to join forces?'

'There's new money going that way,' Clare Tillitson told Sullivan. 'A few days ago we drove some young cattle out that way, including Eric Finkle's bull.'

'And I saw the new honcho's wallet when he hired us – it was stuffed full of greenbacks, Mr Sullivan. Hundreds of dollars. Where'd he get it?'

Sullivan had heard another story about that money and where it might have come from, but it seemed totally ridiculous. The lady had supposedly hit a noted outlaw on the head with an iron skillet and claimed the bounty. Would a man like Hiram Walsh ever have let himself get that careless? It seemed very doubtful. The tale was circulating because it made a good story, that was all.

'These new-hires on the RU. What do we know about them?' Cyrus Sullivan asked, growing serious.

'One of them is a rangy old prairie wolf named Benjamin Trout. He used to ramrod the K/K. The question is, why did he quit? The other one is only a scrawny pup called Eddie. I had the idea he worked with Trout on the K/K Ranch.'

'Trout, huh?' Sullivan said. 'I've heard of him – he's supposed to be a tough man.'

'But he's pulling out,' Clarence Tillitson told

the big man. 'He told us both that, didn't he, Jim? Said that he was only staying at the RU until the river was opened up. Maybe he's got some other deal working, I wouldn't know, but he said he was definitely leaving.'

Jim Hicks was nodding his head in eager agreement. 'That's what he told us, Mr Sullivan. So you see, that only leaves the two women and the sprout, this Eddie, out there to watch over the gold.'

'I see,' Sullivan said, pondering deeply. 'And your idea is that we just move in and take over the ranch and the gold strike for ourselves.' Sullivan was figuring risks and cost against possible profit. How much was there to lose, really, even if the report was utterly false?

But there could be much to be gained. Finishing his beer, he set it down on the table top and thought for a few minutes longer.

'How much would it take, Mr Hicks, for your plan to succeed?'

'Very little. Some lumber and screen material when we get to the point where we are ready to mine.' Hicks leaned forward again, hands cupped around his mug. 'For now all we require is two, maybe three, extra men who know how to use their guns and aren't shy about doing so.'

*

When Ben Trout made his way out on to the swayed front porch of the RU ranch house, coffee mug in his hand, Dink had already been long awake and out working. As Ben watched, the young cowhand hied three of the outlander cattle in to be nearer the free-flowing river. Weary, grinning, Dink rode his little dun toward the porch.

'That's three of 'em, Mr Benjamin!' he said with happy pride.

'It can't all be done in a matter of a few days,' Ben Trout said, chilling Dink's eagerness a little. 'The grass is going to need time to come back.'

'Mrs Robinson and I discussed it. I – we – decided that it was better to gather as many cattle as we can now and keep them bunched along the river, even if it meant having to haul in hay from Riverton for forage.'

Ben shrugged. That plan would mean buying an awful lot of hay over the course of a few months, and the cattle would still pick at the sprouts of new green grass, slowing its return. But it was not Ben's business. Beth owned this ranch and Dink was the property manager. Let them do as they wished. Trout knew that they were wasting money when a little patience would settle the situation.

He had spent too many years running the K/K Ranch and having his word taken as gospel, Trout decided. It was not his part to speak up now, as convinced as he was that these people were rushing ahead recklessly.

Hell, he considered, maybe they were right, and Trout's own ways were old ways.

It didn't matter; he was riding out and leaving them to their own conclusions, their own mistakes. He had nothing left to offer the RU.

'Where's the boss lady?' Dink asked with his horse performing its familiar walking-in-circles display of impatience. *Where was Beth?* Ben did not know.

'Abed, I suppose,' he answered. Both men glanced at the eastern sky, knowing it was late for Beth to be lazing about. That was not her custom.

'I'll get back to work,' Dink said, 'I spotted two more long-haired hideouts back along Snake Canyon.'

Snake Canyon? So the local hills and draws were starting to imprint names on Dink's mental geography. The kid was determined to be local, and he would be in no time at this rate.

Half-shrugging, half-sighing, Benjamin Trout went back into the house. He called out twice to Beth but got no response. Maybe that was for the best. He meant to offer his 'resignation' today. He could do no more here; nothing that Dink couldn't accomplish.

He wandered to his room, pulled his bed-roll from under his bunk and retrieved his kitbag from the shelf in the small closet. To reassure himself he opened his wallet and thumbed through the bills there. Pocketing that, he gathered his shaving gear from beside the washbasin. It was then that he heard the faint murmuring, almost like a child complaining in its sleep. Pausing, he lifted his head toward the sound. It came again, as faintly as before. Puzzled, he started in that direction.

Four steps down the short, dark hall, he could see that Beth's door stood ajar. A little light filtered through the crack. When the mewling sound came again, he could tell that it came from within.

Ben tapped on the door frame and entered. Beth lay in her bed, her dark hair disarranged so that part of it fell across her pale face as if it had trickled there. She was propped up on two pillows, wearing a sort of pale-blue chemise or bed gown – Ben had never learned the proper terminology for ladies' wear. It had no sleeves and her smooth arms looked pale and thin just then.

'Are you all right?' Ben asked foolishly, as people do at such times.

'I will be,' Beth answered with a short-lived smile. 'I'm tired, that's all. There's been a lot of stress around here, going back to our excursion to Hinkley's Ridge. At the time selling those two steers was the only thing that stood between us and starvation.'

Ben nodded his understanding. 'Do you want me to call Minna for you?'

'No. There's nothing she can do. Why ruin her day? She's out there chatting and laughing with Eddie. I'm glad that young man came over here. Minna's never had any friends, male or female, her own age to be with. Just sit and talk to me awhile, will you, Ben?'

'Sure,' he said. Looking around, he noticed there wasn't a chair in the room. Beth patted the bed near her head. She wiped back a few errant strands of hair and again tried a smile.

Ben removed his hat and sat near her. Beth made an effort to sit up straighter, failed and tilted over, her head coming to rest on Benjamin Trout's chest. Without conscious thought he looped his arms around her and held her upright against him. He was now aware of the soap and water, powder and perfume scent of the woman and it troubled him not a little.

Beth only sat with her back against him, saying nothing for a long time. He could feel the pulse in her body; having her there like that, holding her, was distantly comforting to him – and not so distantly a little disturbing.

The door to the bedroom swung open and standing in the doorway were Minna, in her riding togs, and a hatless Dink. Both were a little stunned to see Ben Trout sitting on the woman's bed holding Beth in her nightclothes.

'We were just wondering where. . . .' Dink began, but Ben Trout's growl cut him off.

'Get out of here!' he yelled, partly out of embarrassment.

Minna's face clouded. It seemed as if she were ready to cry. Dink looked a little shaken too. He took Minna's arm and tugged her away.

Beth was silent for a moment, then burst out laughing. 'Aren't you masterful?'

'It was an unexpected interruption at the wrong moment,' Ben said, feeling slightly foolish.

'That's all right. I'll talk to Minna later.'

Ben Trout felt suddenly that it was time to ride. Untangling himself gently, he got to his feet.

'I've gotten too used to you, Ben,' Beth told him as he reached for his hat. 'Too used to having you around in too short a time.'

There was no answer to that and so Ben said nothing. He stood in the middle of the room, just watching Beth, who now had her eyes closed. He knew pretty much what she was going to say next, and found that it did not bother him when she did.

'I shouldn't dare to ask you this, Ben . . . but is there any way you could see your way to staying around here for a little while longer – just until I'm feeling better and back on my feet again?'

'I wouldn't leave you while you're in bed and feeling poorly,' Ben said, and he felt an odd sense of relief as he said it.

'Thank you,' she answered in a faint murmur. 'Thank you, Mr Benjamin.'

There was a tap at the door and Ben turned angrily that way to find Dink again standing there. 'I thought. . . .' Ben said.

'I'm sorry, Mr Benjamin, Mrs Robinson, but this is something else. There's a man in the yard who's drifted in. He says he's looking for work.'

'Why didn't you just tell him that we've got no money to pay anybody any wages?' Ben asked.

'I didn't think it was my place to do that. The RU isn't my ranch.'

'No,' Ben said.

'I thought I should at least ask the boss,' he said, nodding at Beth, who had her blankets pulled up to her chin now.

'I'll go out and see him,' Ben said. 'What do you want me to tell him, Beth?'

'Whatever you think is right, Mr Benjamin,' Beth said. Was she smiling behind her blanket? 'We can afford a man for a few days. If you men plan to start gathering some of our stray cattle or building feeder dams, we could use some help. The man may even be willing to work for room and board. Maybe you can work out some kind of deal. You must use your own judgment, Mr Benjamin.'

Dink was looking from one of them to the other, wondering. Ben positioned his hat, and without smiling or looking at either of them again, he went out.

The man sitting in the shade on the porch, holding the reins to his old gray horse, was of a type usually seen sitting in saloons cadging drinks. He wore a reddish, narrow-brimmed hat with the crown pushed up to form a sort of uneven cone, run-down boots and a blue shirt torn out at one elbow. His jeans were badly sun-faded and Ben would have bet they were nearly out at the seat. He had the narrow, bony face of a New Englander and hopeful, watery-blue eyes.

'How do you do?' the scrawny man said, rising. Ben accepted his proffered hand, which was horny, gripping his firmly. 'My name is Robin Stoker. I've been dragging the line forever, looking for a place where I could find work. The young man, he said he didn't know if you were hiring or not.'

'What can you do, Mr Stoker?'

'I can work cattle or do about anything else you need done,' the man said, his eyes growing hopeful.

'Ever built a spreader dam?' Ben asked.

'Sure I have. Is that what you're planning on doing?'

'I was just asking,' Ben told him. 'Tell me this, what brought you out to the RU looking for a job?'

'It's just that I need work so bad. Then there was these two young men in town who were saying they had worked out here for a few days and been treated right.'

Hicks and Tillitson. Ben told Robin Stoker, 'Here's the thing, Mr Stoker: we're pretty cash-poor just now, and I don't know if we can afford to take on a full-time hand.'

'Oh, no,' Stoker said unhappily. He almost pleaded as he said, 'I'll accept part-time wages, anything. Here's my situation, mister: I've got my wife, Cora, on her way out here from Fort Worth, and I've just got to have some kind of cash in my pockets to take care of her until I can find a real position. I'll do anything at all.' The man's eyes were begging. Ben felt sorry for him, but didn't know what they could do to help Stoker. He took a deep breath. 'Let me talk to the owner again.'

Ben went back into the house. He felt like he always had felt back on the K/K when they had had to turn away a man who was only looking for honest work. Stoker did not look particularly strong, but he was eager for a chance, that was certain.

In Beth's room he found both Minna and Dink

again. They had dragged in a couple of chairs from somewhere and sat looking up at Ben.

'Well?' Beth asked from under her bedclothes. 'What did you tell the man?'

'Nothing yet,' Ben said. 'I don't know what I'm supposed to do.' He looked at Dink and then back at Beth. 'The man says that the ranch manager didn't know what to say. And the owner doesn't know what to tell him. Who exactly is in charge of this ranch?'

'Why, Mr Benjamin,' Beth said in a small voice, 'I thought that was pretty obvious to everyone. It's you who are in charge of the RU, of course.'

NINE

His mood tangled, Ben Trout went back outside to deal with the stranger. It had seemed for a moment inside that all three of them were smiling as he went out of Beth's room. Was this what Beth Robinson had been angling for from the beginning, he wondered, or was it all just chance? He didn't want to attribute false conceptions which might have been all in his mind to Beth, but it did give him pause to wonder. Again.

With Beth's agreement he had come up with a plan the desperate Robin Stoker might be willing to accept. He put it to the man now.

'We just can't afford to hire a man full-time just now,' Ben told him, 'but here's what we're willing to do: room and board and half-pay, plus something we do have plenty of. You say your wife is coming out here without money and no place to stay. The owner of the ranch is willing to deed you a quarter of an acre of land anywhere you like on the property. Even at half-pay you should be able to earn enough to purchase building supplies and get started putting up some sort of shelter on the land.'

'Why, mister, that is generous of you,' Robin said, affected by the offer.

'It won't make you a rich man,' Ben said, 'but it should solve your basic problems for the time being. The boss-lady also said that if Cora should arrive before you've made progress on a place to live, she'll be welcome to stay in the big house for a while.'

Robin's dolorous face had brightened. He thanked Ben at least three more times and asked that his thanks be passed on to Beth. 'Mr Benjamin,' the narrow man said with what seemed to be deep sincerity, 'you'll never get less than my best effort and a full day's work, I promise you that. Yes, sir, the ranch has my gratitude. From now on I ride for the RU brand, and proudly.'

Jim Hicks was meeting again with the money man, Cyrus Sullivan. Clare had gotten himself too drunk the night before to attend.

'Is your friend, Clarence, always this unreliable?' Sullivan demanded.

'No, this is rare. We put in a few hard days out

on the RU, Mr Sullivan. When it comes time, Clare will be there to be counted on.'

'What is it that prompted you to call me over here, Hicks? You know that I don't think it is a good idea for us to be seen together this much.'

'There have been a few developments,' Jim Hicks said, looking up as two cowboys pushed through the saloon door, letting a spray of after-noon sunlight into the room. 'So I was wondering if you had any luck getting a crew together yet.'

'I can get a crew together at any time, day or night, don't worry about that,' Sullivan told him. He leaned forward. 'What about these developments you're talking about? What exactly do you mean?'

'For one thing, Benjamin Trout is still on the RU. I was out looking the place over this morning, watching to see what was up.'

'You told me that Trout was riding out,' Sullivan said, unhappy with the news.

'That's what he told us. Maybe he changed his mind.'

'Or maybe he was lying to you,' Sullivan suggested.

'That could be, I suppose.'

'There's something else you have to tell me?'

'Yes, sir. While I was watching the RU house from the top of the ridge I saw another man arrive.'

'What man?' Sullivan demanded, now frowning.

'I can't tell you. I couldn't recognize him at that distance,' Hicks said. 'I saw the kid take him up to the house and after a while Ben Trout came out. Then Trout went back into the house. When he came back out he shook hands with the man. They talked for a minute more, then the new arrival tied up his horse and Trout led him along to the kitchen at the back of the house. Looked like they were going to feed him.'

Sullivan ignored this irrelevant deduction. He said, 'So it looks like they're bulking up their man-power.'

'That's the way it seemed to me, with Trout staying on and this new man arriving – and he might not be the last to trail in.'

'No.' Cyrus Sullivan was mulling it over. The front door to the saloon was nudged open again and the fleshy face of Sheriff Charlie Stout could be seen peering in, looking for any trouble-makers.

Sullivan rose hurriedly from his seat. He meant it when he had said that he did not want to be seen around Hicks or Clare Tillitson. Whatever he himself decided to do, Sullivan felt sure that the two younger men were going to get up to some devilry and he did not wish to be associated with it. He and Sheriff Stout had had some discussions in the past, most of them unpleasant. Cyrus Sullivan was comfortably well off, probably the wealthiest man in Riverton. At this time of life he did not wish to risk more trouble on what might have been a pipe dream.

On the other hand if there was a rich strike of gold on the RU and it could be taken over as easily as Hicks believed, Sullivan was not about to pass it up.

'It seems to me,' Hicks, who had now also risen, said, 'that the best thing for us to do is make our play as soon as possible. We don't know what Ben Trout has in mind. We can't have him gathering a crew and fortifying the place.'

'No,' was all Sullivan said, still glancing toward the door where the sheriff had been.

'I mean – it could be that Trout has it in mind to send for some of his old friends from the K/K. It wouldn't take them that long to ride to the RU.'

'No,' Sullivan said. He hated to admit it but Jim Hicks was probably right. If they were going to make their move it was better to do it sooner rather than later when something might change to tilt matters in the RU's favor.

There was always Aaron McCluskey, Sullivan was thinking as he stepped outside into the harsh sunlight. McCluskey was hardly Sullivan's favorite person to work with, but he and his crew did fit

109

Hicks's description of the type of men they needed: men who knew guns and were not shy about using them.

Aaron McCluskey was hardly the shy type.

The only wonder was that the sly man from Utah hadn't been hanged yet or locked up in prison. Sheriff Stout would like to haul him in, certainly, but McCluskey was always careful to wear his best manners when he put his town suit on. Outside of town, as Sullivan had discovered after it was too late, the man was a butcher. But as long as he was paid. . . . Yes, Sullivan thought as he started for home, McCluskey was his man. He would tell the bandit to have his men ready to ride.

There was no point in starting any major new projects with what was left of the day. Instead, Ben sent Dink and Robin out doing what he had already done: counting the stray cattle. Dink would be able to fill Robin in on the boundaries of the RU; at the same time Robin Stoker could be on the lookout for his promised home site. There really was no good spot for a house that Ben knew of away from the river, but perhaps Robin had privacy in mind.

'I can't believe that little man actually has a wife,' Minna said as she and Beth, who seemed to have recovered rapidly, darted about rearranging the kitchen while Ben watched.

'Or that he would bring her out with absolutely nothing prepared,' Beth said.

'Nothing is all he had,' Ben Trout reminded them.

Minna had stopped working to lean against the sink. 'What must she look like to have married a man like Robin Stoker!' the pretty little blonde said.

Ben was growing tired of the unkind speculation. He said in a low voice, 'There's someone for everyone, Minna.'

'Yes,' Beth agreed instantly. 'That's what they say, Minna, and it seems to be true. There's someone for everybody.'

Beth was looking directly at Ben Trout when she said that, and reasonably or not it caused him to feel uncomfortable. He rose and left the kitchen.

Outside it was clear and very warm; a dry breeze stirred the cottonwood trees. In a sullen mood for no particular reason, Ben Trout walked out to take a look at what they had started to call 'the yard cows', meaning those which had not been driven in from the hills, but planted next to the river and left there to do as they liked. Prominent among them and of the most interest to Ben was the black bull. Minna called it 'Toro' which made sense but was a little unimaginative.

The bull, free to examine the cows closely now,

was raising only contempt, or at best lethargy, from the heifers. The animals, placid though they were, could nevertheless display irritation with Toro, who was constantly snuffling at them. The truth was the cows were just too young; times would change for Toro.

None of the yard cows showed any wounds or signs of illness. They were spared the nicks and maladies common to open-range stock. Of the steers that Dink had overeagerly driven in, one had wounds on its shoulder of the type a cow got from barbed wire although there was no wire strung on the RU. Cactus, then, Ben guessed. The other two appeared to be in good shape; hopefully none carried parasites. They would have to be watched as would any other newcomers brought in from the hills. They could afford to have no parasite-borne illnesses on the ranch like the quick-spreading Texas fever. That would ruin the RU before it even had a chance to get started again.

Ben rose from examining a cow's hock, wiped his hands on his jeans and removed his hat. Taking a deep breath, he let his eyes scan the dark hills surrounding the basin. He paused.

Just for a moment he thought he had seen a man up there where none belonged, at the near end of the road to Riverton. And for just a moment he had thought he recognized the red-plaid shirt the man was wearing.

A shirt very like the one that Jim Hicks habitually wore.

Squinting into the glare of the sunlight, Ben found that he could no longer be sure that there was a man there. The shadows had combined to conceal him – if man it was. Perhaps he had been thinking of Hicks and his vow to return to the RU and provided his imaginary man with Hicks's shirt. The mind plays funny games.

If it were Hicks, Ben thought as he walked toward the barn and his sorrel horse, what did he want there, and why did he not just ride in? There was Minna, of course, and perhaps the man was waiting for a chance to see her when no one else would know. Hicks could be thinking like that. The human mind plays all sorts of games, sets up scenes which are never acted out except in imagination.

Ben did not think that his own theater of the mind was accurate. A girl of Minna's age could only cause trouble for a young buck like Hicks, and he undoubtedly knew that. He had been looking at Minna simply because she was there when he was.

He reached the barn and began to saddle his horse, still deep in thought. If it had been Hicks, what could he possibly want, then? Four cows and an ornery young bull? Not likely. But what else had they?

A ridiculous-seeming notion that Ben had had before returned to him. It still made no sense to him, but it had sheltered in his chest and grown stronger over the past few days until it seemed almost logical.

Dropping the reins to his sorrel, Ben tramped back over to the house where he found Beth alone in the kitchen. Entering, he let the spring door slam behind him. She looked up at him from where she worked, pouring a bag of flour into a canister. Her face was wreathed in questions. The look on Ben Trout's face puzzled and alarmed her.

'What is it, Ben? What's the matter?'

'Mrs Robinson,' Ben said in a seldom-used gruff tone, 'there are some men who are after your gold mine.'

'Have you had too much sun, Ben? I have no gold mine, and you know it.'

'Yes, I know it,' he said, sitting on the corner of the kitchen table, 'but they don't.'

'This is. . . .' she stuttered and fumbled for a word, 'preposterous.'

'Yes,' he agreed.

'Absurd!'

'You are correct,' Ben told her. 'I've already had this conversation with myself.'

'Then why; then what. . . ?' Flustered, she spilled some flour on the floor.

'If enough people repeat a lie, it becomes the truth to some of them,' Ben said, shifting slightly. 'Look, there are people in Hinkley's Ridge who know that you have purchased supplies with gold dust. You even told me that there were rumors there about you having made a gold strike out here.'

'Yes, but. . . .' a frustrated Beth began. Ben Trout held up his hand.

'In Riverton you are known as the women with the gold mine. Sheriff Stout referred to you that way. The rumor must have gotten around all over that town. In fact when I hired those two men to work out here, one of them – Hicks – asked me if it involved dangerous work, like in a mine shaft.'

'Still!' Beth exclaimed. Now she was laughing.

'I know,' Ben said, 'I know – I told you I've already had this discussion with myself more than once.

'Don't you see,' he said, 'the next thing that happens is we go into Riverton to buy a ton of supplies and some cattle. If you are supposed to be so dirt poor, where did we get the money?'

'You know where, it was thanks to the bad man,

Hiram Walsh.'

'Yes,' Ben said, holding up his hand for patience again, 'but then there is the river.'

'The river?'

'Unblocking it as we did. People won't believe that we did it for the benefit of the few scraggly cattle you are running on the RU. They may even believe that we purchased the new cows as a diversion, to keep people from thinking about what we really intended to use the increased water supply for.'

'Which would be?' Beth asked, no longer smiling.

'As you probably know there are certain types of gold mining which require large amounts of water. I think that's what Hicks and Clare thought we were working at. I think they jumped to a conclusion based on rumors and now the rumor has grown and spread.'

'But it's all so preposterous!' Beth said again. 'Ben, we must talk to these people and tell them that it's all untrue.'

Ben rose and looked down at her, his face grim. 'That's the second thing we must do, you're right.'

'The second?' Beth was again dismayed. 'Then what is the first thing we must do? Tell me, Ben.'

'We'd better fort up, because I have an idea we're going to have a horde of gold-seekers overrunning the RU, and they'll be chasing their dreams with wild eyes and guns, unwilling to listen to reason until it's too late.'

TEN

'Can't we send for the county sheriff?' Minna asked as they all sat in a circle that evening in the living room discussing the situation.

'No,' Ben answered, 'we can't expect Sheriff Stout to ride out here on unfounded suspicion.'

'You're right,' Dink said. 'Whatever there is to take care of, we'll have to do it ourselves.'

'Yes, I think so,' Ben agreed 'Except for you, Robin,' he said, settling his gaze on the bulbous-nosed, scrawny man. 'You just arrived and you may have ridden into a hornets' nest, certainly not what you had in mind. You're free to leave and no one will think the less of you for it.'

'Not on your life!' Robin Stoker said stoutly. 'I didn't hire on with a promise that all would be sweetness and light. I ride for the brand. I'm an RU man now.'

'All right,' Ben Trout said with a smile. 'Here's what I think we should do. Dink, find a good lookout point in the hills behind the house. We'll have to keep a man up there day and night. And every man carry his Winchester at all times. It won't do to get caught unprepared.'

'What do we do in the meantime while we're waiting for the storm to break?' Robin asked. The older man now looked worried. Perhaps he was concerned about bringing his wife into a mess like this.

'What we can do. We meant to start on those spreader dams sooner or later. Now seems to be the time. Let's get this valley ready for a crop of spring grass.'

When the others were gone – Dink to search the hills for a good lookout spot, Minna to her room and Robin Stoker to collect shovels and picks for the work of the day – Beth asked Ben Trout, 'Do you think we are really about to come under attack?'

'I just don't know,' Ben admitted. 'But it's better to be safe than sorry, don't you think? Men will do wild things for gold or the promise of it – I've seen it before.'

They stood in the doorway now, looking out at the dry yellow valley floor, holder of wishes, promises, rebirth and bloody war all at once. Beth must have been thinking of some of these things as well. She had been looking down, but now she raised her bright eyes to his.

'Do you think. . . ? Maybe someone should ride into Riverton and gauge the mood of the town. Even talk to Sheriff Stout and explain our concerns. I could do that.'

'No,' Ben said immediately and stiffly. 'We can't risk it. You could find yourself a hostage, and where would that leave us?'

Beth did not argue; she sighed. 'I didn't like the idea much myself, but I thought it was worth kicking around. Tell me, Ben, who are we really afraid of? The way you are thinking we only have the two men we hired to work out here, Hicks and Clare, who may have gotten the wrong idea of what we were up to.'

'And whoever they may have carried the tale to on some drunken night.'

'Even so – you're talking about a shiftless bunch of saloon rabble there. They'd be unwilling to leave their usual ways for something that required effort.'

'We don't know who they know in town. In Riverton, I only know three or four people,' Ben said. 'I have no idea what goes on there. Hicks and Clare may have other friends, men with more money, power and ambition.'

'They may,' Beth answered, 'but would men like that be willing to risk all on the word of two saddle tramps?'

'Gold rushes have started on less evidence,' Ben told her. 'The reason is clear – these men have no jobs or only poor jobs; gold holds a promise of wealth and ease – though the reality is usually far different.'

'I still say we have little to fear from two casual laborers,' Beth said as if trying to convince herself.

'What about Hiram Walsh?' Ben asked and Beth's voice stuttered to a stop.

'Why would you bring him up?' she asked.

'We never found out why Walsh was on the RU, what he wanted. He may have heard rumors of a gold strike back in Hinkley's Ridge and come out to have a look for himself. At the time, if you remember, we asked ourselves if the outlaw was riding alone. Maybe he was not, and by now the rest of his gang is wondering why he did not return.'

'Oh, dear,' Beth said with almost painful under-standing. She turned and looked up at him again. Robin Stoker had pulled up in front of the house with the wagon and work tools. 'All of this is only speculation, is it not, Ben? We don't know if anyone is really interested in the poor RU.'

'No. No, we don't.'

She stared out the door in silence. 'Poor little patch of ground bringing so much sorrow to everyone.'

He did not want to let Beth worry so much that she might fall ill again, and so he told her that they were probably wrong, and anyway they had their defensive plans in place. Beth's face contained a trusting look and she stretched forward to lightly kiss Ben before walking away toward the kitchen. It was obvious that she didn't believe Ben's assurances.

Nor did Ben Trout trust them himself.

He scuffled across the porch to join an eager Robin Stoker on the wagon, only once allowing himself a look back at the house where a heavy-hearted woman on the brink of defeat waited.

It was nearly dusk when Benjamin Trout called a halt to the day's work on the spreader dam, which in his estimation was going well. The river water would be slowed and diverted to fan out and nourish the new grass when it came. The river still flowed strong and smoothly. In his mind Ben could still envision all of this paying off in the end: green grass, young cows, a healthy ranch.

If the destroyers did not come.

He rode off to find Dink, to relieve him. Robin had been assigned the late-night shift which the man did not object to. 'I'm the new-hire,' was his only comment about the situation. 'Got to expect that.'

Dink was in more of a complaining mood when Ben found him in a tight little rocky nook high on the near hills. 'About time. I come up here without so much as a sandwich.'

Ben avoided telling the kid that that was his own fault. Ben himself had two thick sandwiches, one of fried eggs, the other of ham, which Beth had made for him.

'You'll get your supper. Seen anyone around?'

'Not a soul.'

'Good, let's hope it stays that way.' It was going to be a long, endless night, Ben knew. There was a half-moon rising in an hour or so, but still the hours of staring into the empty canyons and across the long, dark land could produce night-ghosts, and Ben needed none of those.

'I don't think they'll come at night,' Ben said to Dink, but maybe he was only trying to reassure himself. 'But keep your rifle handy.'

'I mean to, Mr Benjamin, I surely mean to.'

It was a long, cold and dreary night for Ben Trout. He saw no one but a prowling coyote who seemed to be drawn by the scent of his sandwiches and was easily shooed away. Robin arrived promptly to relieve him, his face beaming, his own pockets stuffed with food. Ben told him about the scavenging coyote. There was nothing else to report, for which he was thankful.

At breakfast Robin and Trout discussed the spreader dams and a few other trivial matters. Dink had relieved Robin at his post just after dawn and was now standing watch on the hill.

'I made sure that Eddie took some food with him today,' Minna said with what seemed to be some pride.

Beth sat at the table with a cup of coffee. 'Ben,' she said, earnestly, 'as quiet as it has been, don't you think that there's a chance we both over-reacted to our fears?'

'Of course I do,' Ben said. 'In fact, I hope that's the case.'

'So do I,' Robin Stoker said, sipping coffee from his own cup. 'I'd really hate to have Cora land in the middle of this trouble.'

'Of course you would,' Beth said. 'Tell me, have you heard from your wife?'

'There ain't no way I could have,' Robin shrugged. 'I'll just have to wait and hope for her.'

'Have you found a home site yet?' Beth asked.

'If you don't mind, ma'am,' Robin told her, 'there's a little pocket valley not far north of where the river had to be widened out. There's three or four oak trees standing there, and good water of course. I thought it might do just fine.'

'You're welcome to it,' Beth said. 'It was part of our agreement.'

'When things settle down,' Ben offered, 'Dink and I can help you with the framing.'

'Assuming I can afford the lumber.'

'Maybe we can advance you a little on your wages,' Beth said, despite the look that she got from Ben telling her she still needed to watch her money. Actually neither believed it to be a great risk. A man who wants to build a house and settle in with his wife isn't going to fork his horse and ride off in the middle of the night.

Ben pushed his coffee cup away and the two men started off to work on the dam again. In the late afternoon Ben left Robin to it and took his sorrel to ride up to relieve Dink at lookout.

'How long are we going to keep this up?' Dink asked.

'The watching? Until we can feel fairly secure.'

'I don't care for it. It's like being under siege.'

'Isn't it? Well, Dink, I'm thinking that the longer it takes the better chance there is that cooler heads have prevailed and they've called off any plans they might have had.'

'Or maybe the cooler heads have just had the time by now to lay their plans more carefully,' Dink said dourly.

'That's why we're still here,' Ben said, unsaddling his horse. 'I don't like it any more than you do, but it only seems prudent.'

Dink swung aboard his dun pony with a grin. 'And to think, Mr Benjamin, you could have nearly been in Tucson by now.'

'It's an uncertain trail we all ride,' Ben said, settling into the shade, his eyes even now lifting to the far hills where he had previously seen the prowling man.

The sun was warm. Not a breath of air stirred in the rocky cleft they had chosen for their lookout point. The air smelled of sage and dust, nothing more. As the sun fell lower it was difficult not to grow sleepy with the warmth and inactivity. Ben tried playing mental games on himself. Most of these led him to Beth Robinson.

Ben did not fall asleep; he forced himself to remain as alert as he could, but by the time Robin Stoker arrived to relieve him, he had drifted into a dull lethargy and definitely needed to be relieved.

'Nothing, boss?' Robin asked.

'You didn't hear any shots, did you?' Ben asked, rising as the scrawny man swung down from his horse.

'No,' Robin answered with a smile.

'How's the dam coming?' Ben asked.

'I'd say we need another fifty feet or so. You tell

me what you think tomorrow.'

Ben nodded and yawned, turning his horse's head toward the house. He was hungry and tired, and deserved to be both. Robin was in for another uncomfortable night, but Ben could do nothing about that. At least the little man had his wife to think about, that and the new house he was hoping to build. That was more than Ben had, he reflected as he rode along the narrow trail.

Robin would be safe in his hidden nook. As Ben had told Dink, it was unlikely that the raiders – if there were any – would come at night.

It took five more minutes along the trail to prove Ben Trout wrong.

ELEVEN

Three gunshots racketed out in rapid succession from near the lookout post Ben had just quitted. His horse reared in fright at the report of the shots rising from out of the dark night and Ben tried to calm the sorrel and spin it on its heels at the same time as yet another near shot roared in the stillness of the darkening night.

Ben leaned low across the withers and flagged his horse with his hat uphill again, toward the thunder of the guns. At the same time he cursed himself. As the leader of these men, he should have been enough of a general to realize that they could not continue to use the exact same spot for their lookout post. It should have moved around, been varied enough to make any attacker uncertain of its location. Recriminations were of no use now. Ben continued his uphill charge, Colt in hand.

A man popped up from behind a screen of road-side sumac and Ben shot him dead without aiming, without thinking. The attacker stumbled back, slipped and fell on to his face to slide down the hill over the rough gravel.

From above, one final shot was fired, this one aimed at Ben Trout. Going to the side of his horse Ben fired back blindly but heard the grunt of a man as if he had been struck by flying lead. That was followed by hurried, stumbling footsteps as a man broke for the concealing brush.

Ben Trout burst into the cleft in the hill which served as their lookout post, surprised and pleased that Robin's old gray horse had stood its ground and not fled in the excitement. He would need the horse, because Robin Stoker had not been so for-tunate.

The narrow man sat against the wall of the cave, rifle across his lap. He was holding his leg, which was bleeding freely. There was also blood showing on the shoulder of his shirt.

'Any more around, Robin?' Ben asked.

'I couldn't tell you, boss. All I seen was them two – they were enough to do the job on me.'

'Hold on. I'll get you back to the house. Can you sit on your horse?'

'I guess I'd better if I want to go along,' Robin said.

'I guess you'd better,' Ben said with an uneasy grin. There was no point in even trying any first aid with the house so near. Beth would have more available tools. With a deal of effort Ben managed to help Robin on to his horse's back and they started down the trail again, Ben's eyes shifting from point to shadowy point warily, Robin reeling in the saddle beside him.

The shots had alerted the house. Dink met them at the door in shirtsleeves, carrying his Winchester. He started to ask questions of Ben, but Trout told him: 'Give me a hand getting Robin into the house.'

Keeping a watch, Ben had still seen no other trespassers. No lurkers prowled in the shadows, no armed horsemen charged the house. The attack, if that was what it was, seemed strangely uncoordinated.

Together Ben and Dink got the badly wounded Robin Stoker from his horse's back and into the house where a frightened Minna and concerned Beth waited.

'Find some clean cloths, Minna,' Beth said, immediately taking charge of things. For the time being Robin was stretched out on the sofa and Beth began cutting away material from his pant leg and shirt with her scissors. Robin seemed to have already passed into unconsciousness. Minna had returned with strips of clean white muslin.

'Carbolic and hot water,' Beth ordered without looking up from her task.

'Is it bad?' Dink asked Ben.

'Pretty bad, I'd say.'

'What happened?' Dink asked in a lowered voice, turning toward the front door with Ben beside him.

'Two men jumped him up on the hill. I got one for sure; the other ran off into the brush, hit.'

'Did you recognize them?'

'I didn't have the time to try to identify them,' Ben told the kid.

Beth, who had paused briefly as she waited for Minna to return, had been listening. 'Was it our two, Ben?' she asked, meaning Jim Hicks and Clare Tillitson.

'I just don't know.' Ben had not even a recollection of how the two men had been built. The episode had just been a blurred flurry of night-shadowed action. 'It could have been, I suppose.'

'If it was them,' Beth continued, 'and you got both of them, that could mean our troubles are over, that it was just those two making trouble.'

'Maybe,' he said to appease Beth. He, himself, did not believe that the night's action had been the end to anything, but only the prelude for what was to come. Another minute proved him right.

'Riders coming in!' Dink said, closing the front door. 'Three of them to the east, another two to the west.'

Ben Trout went to the window and knelt down, returning his attention to the world outside. He could now see the distant incoming riders in the hesitant moonlight. They had not fired yet, proba- bly because the range was long. Beth was working on Robin's wounded leg, Minna assisting her. They were boxed in good and proper. The same thought had occurred to Dink.

'I can slip out there and take up a post in the shadows of the trees. They won't be able to see me if I go now and we douse the lantern.'

'I need that lantern light!' Beth complained.

'Then out the back door,' Dink said. 'We're all trapped here.'

'No,' Ben said, having made his decision. He stood and put his hand on Dink's shoulder. 'Stay here and keep your eye out the window.'

'Ben, where are you going to go?' Dink asked desolately.

'Why, out the back door,' Ben Trout answered with a grin. 'You had the right idea, Dink, but the wrong man.'

Beth's eyes looked up to follow him across the room as she continued to work on the pale Robin Stoker's wounds. She looked hopeful and fearful at once, as she had every right to be. Whatever either of them had thought of the night raid previously, it had not been a mad excursion by two deluded hired hands, but a frontal assault by an organized band. Who their leader was, how good a general he might prove to be, was the question. So far the assault had looked fairly uncoordinated, but who knew if the man had more tricks up his sleeve.

Fighting a last-ditch defensive battle with two women and a wounded man to consider was not Ben Trout's sort of war.

The sharp crack of a Winchester rifle sounded across the stillness of the night before Ben had reached his intended position of concealment among the cottonwood trees. The stab of flame he saw across the distances indicated that it was one of the incoming riders, perhaps jittery, overeager, who had fired first at great range. Ben had time to count to five, to wind his way toward the trees, before the snap of an answering shot from within the house indicated that Dink had been tracking the rider with his sights. From his position, Ben could see the bad man slap at his chest and then tumble from his saddle as his horse danced away.

The other outlaws would be more cautious.

Ben was braced beyond the large cottonwood tree he had reached, planning his next move. His targets, lost in the night, could not be easily tracked, whereas the night riders had the lighted house as their obvious target. The lantern within the house was dim, but still it was plain to see its outlines. With no light at all, those inside would not have been able to move around. Beth would have to abandon her attempt to save the badly injured Robin Stoker. That, he knew, she would not do.

At the sound of an approaching horse, Ben pressed his back more firmly against the trunk of the tree, holding his Winchester with the barrel pointed up. A bead of perspiration trickled into his eye, stinging it. Ben did not dare move even to wipe it away. The horse was nearly to him. Now he could see its shadow, dimly cast by the dying moon and the stars.

Something was wrong . . . and then he knew what it was. Ben hit the ground and rolled away as two shots were fired at him. The shadow he had seen had shown no horse's rider. The man had dismounted and sent his pony past Ben's hiding place to try to draw him out of shelter.

Now, positioned on one knee, Ben did see his target and he raised the rifle muzzle for a snap shot on the running man. The rifle cracked, bucked against his shoulder and his target crumpled up.

Looking around the yard, which seemed otherwise still, Ben moved in a crouch toward his victim. Lying on his back was a heavy man with eyes open to the night. He blinked at Ben Trout.

'Seen that trick before, have you?' the wounded raider asked. 'I learned it from the Indians. It'll generally fool a man.'

'Nothing works every time,' Ben said, crouching down to yank the man's revolver from his holster and hurl it away into the shadows.

'I wasn't planning on using that, mister,' the wounded man told Ben. 'I'm bad hit; I got no more fight left in me.'

'Who sent you out here?' Ben Trout wanted to know, not forgetting to keep his eyes on the darkness.

'Who?' the man said in a weak voice as if he was having trouble remembering or forming words.

'Who paid you for this job?' Ben demanded in a voice too loud for the situation.

'Paid me. . . ?' the man remained hesitant. Not out of loyalty, Ben thought, but only because he was working with a failing mind. 'It was Cyrus Sullivan who hired us,' the man said, barely moving his lips.

'Sullivan? I don't know him.'

'Then you don't know Riverton,' the bad man said feebly. 'Everyone knows who Mr Sullivan is. . . .' Then he said no more, could say no more. Ben got to his feet, waiting for a moment as he thought that here was another man who had died over nothing, the myth of a gold mine which did not exist.

He strode back toward the house, then ducked and scurried for its cover as two rifle shots sounded from the other end of the house and were answered by two timed shots from Dink's rifle within. Distantly another man's horse raced free across the valley. Had Dink gotten one of them? It seemed so. The outlaws' haphazard attack had been ill-conceived and ill-planned. Carried out by a group of men with no real heart for the job, possibly mostly drunk. It seemed a half-hearted affair, enough to earn them a night's pay when they returned. . . .

To Riverton. *To Cyrus Sullivan*, who would now be convinced to give it up after the result of this raid, or possibly thinking that he had not sent enough men, enough of the experienced type he needed to pull off the attack, and send back a larger army. Ben had never met the man; he couldn't guess how Sullivan might react.

Ben called out softly before he entered the back door of the house. It was a good thing that he had. A shaky-looking Beth Robinson waited in the dark kitchen with that huge Sharps .50 buffalo gun of hers. Her face was ashen, her hands trembled a little.

'We heard a stray shot out there earlier. We didn't know. . . .'

'I got lucky and took my man down,' Ben told her as she leaned up against him, rolling her head from side to side.

Beth looked up with damp eyes. 'But there will be other men, Ben. How many more? How long can we survive this? How long can it go on?'

'I'm going to put an end to it,' he said, holding both of her shoulders.

'How? How can you, Ben?'

'I'll tell you all in a little while. No one else got hit, did they?'

'No, everyone is all right for now. Except poor Robin, of course. He's in terrible shape, Ben. There was only so much we could do for him.'

They made their way to the front room where the dim lantern still glowed, Beth holding her rifle, Ben's arm around her. Dink glanced up from his position at the window.

'How many more are out there, boss?' he asked.

'It wasn't clear; I don't think many. Some of them may have taken to their heels already. Just keep a good watch and keep your rifle fully loaded.'

'Eddie got one of them a few minutes ago,'

Minna said proudly. 'I saw him fall from his horse.' No one responded. Minna, young as she was, still did not seem to realize that men were actually dying out there. On the sofa Robin Stoker's lips fluttered audibly, but he remained blessedly asleep. Beth's bandaging was plain to see on his leg and shoulder.

'You said you were going to put an end to this, Ben,' Beth said, and Dink's eyes turned curiously toward them again. 'Tell us now – how do you intend to do that?'

'How I intend to try to do it,' Ben corrected. 'There's only one way to take care of a rattlesnake. They can bite even after you think they've been killed. You have to cut off the snake's head and bury it.'

'Yes, but. . . .' Beth said uncertainly, unsure of Ben's meaning.

'I know now where the snake's head is, who he is. Do you know a man named Cyrus Sullivan?' Both of the women wagged their heads negatively. 'Well, he seems to be some sort of big shot in Riverton, big enough to afford to launch this war against us. If he's that important, he shouldn't be too hard to find. I intend to go to Riverton and find the man – and cut off the snake's head.'

TWELVE

Riverton hadn't grown or prettified itself any since the last time Ben Trout had seen it. It was neither noisier nor quieter, cleaner nor dirtier than it had been. It simply clung to its tentative existence on the long desert flats as if its tilting buildings and sagging adobes had tenacious roots stretching into the desert soil.

Ben had decided that it was time to talk to Marshal Charles Stout. Now they had good evidence that the RU was under attack. What Stout could do about it was uncertain, but he had to be notified. First, Ben meant to find the one man who could do something about matters: Cyrus Sullivan. At the RU the dying man had indicated that Sullivan was well known in Riverton, perhaps chief among its citizens. He should not be hard to locate. Ben decided to avoid the saloons where some of the gathered men might be on Sullivan's payroll. He had not yet seen Hicks and Clare Tillitson on the ranch, though either or both of them could easily be among the dead men. At any rate he wished to avoid anyone who might recognize him. The general store was still open and Ben started the sorrel in that direction.

Inside the little man who was obviously ready to close down for the night looked up with a sort of expectant fear. Ben lifted a peaceful hand.

'I just dropped in to ask a question: where can I find Mr Cyrus Sullivan? We have a business deal pending.'

The mention of Sullivan seemed to draw the storekeeper's mouth into a tight, sour expression, but he answered readily, probably just to get Ben out of his store. The man walked forward, wiped a hand on his apron and pointed up the street to the west.

'Two-story white house about a quarter of a mile out. You can't miss it.'

'Do you think he'd be at home?' Ben asked. The storekeeper lost patience.

'Mister, I don't know and I couldn't care less where Cyrus Sullivan is.'

Ben touched his hat brim in a gesture of thanks and stepped out again. There was now a little bit of extra noise on the streets of Riverton. It seemed

140

that the crowd had spilled out of one of the saloons on to the street. Ben didn't try to discover what had caused the ruckus – probably a fist fight – but rode past the knot of drinking men without showing his face clearly.

He had no time for their squabbles. He had only one objective on this night.

Stillness returned and the glare of the lanterns fell away as he proceeded up the road. Night birds sang in the oak trees along the way; the dying moon showed the way clearly.

The white house, when he came upon it, was truly impressive for this part of the country. Sitting on a low knoll, surrounded by live oak trees, it had colonnades in front supporting an upstairs portico flanked by two balconies. Behind one of these curved white balconies a lighted window showed, the lamplight shining through dark-green drapes. Sullivan's private office, his bedroom perhaps? There was no telling.

Were there guards around? That was of more concern to Ben just then. He saw no one, but he rode his horse as softly as he could into the shelter of the trees and sat there for long minutes, watching the shadows for any movement. Swinging down after a while, he began making his way toward the rear of the house, his senses still on high alert.

141

No one came forward or called out as he slipped through the shadows toward the back door of the house. It must be the kitchen, he thought, and his guess was reinforced as he passed a pile of slops intended for fertilizer or for hog food. Ben tensed as he stepped up on to the narrow back porch and reached for the doorknob, not knowing what alarm he might raise – a shout or, worse, a sudden blast of gunfire.

The knob turned beneath his hand. The door was open and he slipped into the kitchen, which still smelled of the evening meal. Which way? There was no point in hesitating now. He was committed to his course of action.

Ahead, then; he crossed the room beyond the kitchen and found himself at the foot of a curved stairway faintly illuminated by the burning lamp above. Ben had encountered no guards, meaning Cyrus Sullivan felt perfectly secure alone in his fortress. Sure – he had no reason to cringe and hide like two lonely, fearful women in the desert wilds.

Ben found the lighted upstairs room, and pistol in hand, he toed the door open. The room was all in white with gilt trimming and a high ceiling. The desk behind which Cyrus Sullivan sat was oak, topped with polished cedar. The eyes Sullivan lifted toward Ben were not startled, not angry, but only inquisitive.

'Who are you and what are you doing here?' he asked in an even voice.

'My name's Ben Trout. I've come from the RU to tell you to pull off your men before any more of them get killed.'

'My men?' Sullivan said innocently, spreading his hands.

'That's what I said. You can keep hiring them and having them waste their lives, or quit now. I'm telling you there's no gold on that property and never has been but for a little dust the women gathered in their spare time.'

'I am not going to argue with you,' Sullivan answered. 'I don't think I believe you, Mr Trout. I have my own sources. . . .'

'You have the word of a couple of delusional roustabouts who wouldn't know a gold mine if they fell in one.'

Sullivan made that gesture with his spreading hands again and leaned back a little in his chair. 'Not that I'm admitting anything, Trout, but I haven't got the power to pull those men off the job. Those men you speak of aren't mine. They ride with a man named Aaron McCluskey; maybe you've heard of him.'

'I have,' Ben had to admit. 'He's that cheap little gunhand from down in the Brazos country.'

'Cheap little gunhand?' Sullivan laughed and sputtered. 'He'd take a man like you and spit you out again without even chewing.'

'Maybe. That remains to be seen. Meanwhile I'm telling you to get those men off the RU. We've killed a few, we'll quite likely kill a few more while they're trying to take over a mine that doesn't even exist.'

Sullivan's face turned thoughtful; too thoughtful, Ben decided. 'What I can do. . . .' Sullivan said, reaching for his desk drawer. That was as far as he got with his speech, as far as he meant to go.

From the desk drawer Sullivan pulled a Colt revolver. Ben flung himself to one side before the man had time to sight properly, and the bullet winged its way past him, shattering glass behind him. Braced against the wall, Ben Trout returned fire. His bullet tagged Sullivan just below the vest pocket on his left side, causing Sullivan to fold up, his pistol dropping from his hand to clatter against the floor.

Ben approached the dead man cautiously, his eyes shifting to the door behind him. Sullivan was dead, no doubt about it. Stupid of him. He had McCluskey, his hired gunny, out here ready to earn his wages by fighting it out with Ben or anyone else who got in their way, and yet he had chosen to try to do the job himself, quite clumsily.

'That wasn't smart,' Ben muttered to the dead Cyrus Sullivan. 'Let a man do the job he's hired to.'

Looking both ways, Ben briefly considered making his escape through the window, but he had still not seen another person since entering the house, and going out that way might draw more attention to him than simply walking back through the kitchen and exiting the way he had come in.

Slipping out into the night, which now had gone almost totally black with the moon disappearing beyond the western mountains and the stars covered with a veil of sheer clouds, Ben Trout returned hurriedly but warily to his horse, expecting to find men waiting for him lurking in every shadow, behind every tree.

He encountered none.

He rode back through the unconcerned town of Riverton. He saw no horses that had been hard-ridden in front of the saloons. Where, then, were the raiders who had fled the RU?

Ben Trout again considered trying to find the marshal and telling him what was going on, but balked at the idea of admitting that he had just killed Cyrus Sullivan. This was a small town and there could be some kind of connection between Sullivan and Marshal Stout for all he knew. He did not need to spend a night in jail, at any rate, but to make his way back to the RU as rapidly as possible and see what damage might have been done in his absence.

Turning north toward the ranch he was approached by three men and Ben breathed in deeply to slow his heart rate. These, judging by the direction they were travelling, had to be McCluskey men, raiders coming from the RU.

He decided to risk it – in the nearly coal-black night he drew his horse to the side of the road and waited for the approaching riders.

'Hold it,' he heard one of the men say and they all slowed their horses as they saw Ben on the side of the road, waiting. None of them could know him, and none could recognize him in the dark of night, but that gave him no sense of confidence.

'Who the hell are you?' their leader growled.

'Just a town-hire,' Trout said. 'I was riding out to find my friends when I got the news. Someone killed Cyrus Sullivan – there's no pay coming for this job.'

'What do you mean?' the outlaw demanded gruffly.

'Just what I said. There's nobody to pay the bills now. Any man fighting out there is fighting for nothing.'

'And dammit,' a second raider said, 'Darby got himself killed on this night.'

'Are you sure of this?' their leader demanded of Ben.

'You can ask anybody once you get back to town,' Ben assured the man. 'I was going out to call my friends off. They only hired on for the money.'

'Chet,' said the third man who had not spoken before, 'you know who's going to be on the boil.'

'Yeah, I know.'

'McCluskey don't like it when things don't go his way. He goes off his anchor and he shoots men, sometimes the wrong men. I've seen it before.'

'So have I,' the man called Chet said.

'So, what do we do?'

'First we go into town and ask around to see if this gent knows what he's talking about,' Chet said with a nod toward Ben Trout. 'If it's true about Sullivan being dead, I've an idea I wouldn't mind riding down to Nogales again just to look around.'

There was a little more conversation that Ben didn't understand, not being familiar with the places or people the raiders knew, but finally they trailed out toward Riverton with a few backward glances. Letting out his breath, Ben struck spurs to the sorrel and lined out toward the RU.

In the still of the night, with the stars now forming a silver blanket across the sky, Ben rode toward the

147

ranch house door, calling out as he arrived. The door opened cautiously at first and then was flung wide as Beth rushed from the house, running toward Ben, who stepped down to greet her as she threw her arms around him and clung tightly to him. Over her shoulder Dink could be seen in the doorway, Minna, cowering slightly, beside him.

'Are they all gone?' Beth asked, looking around Ben. 'All of them?'

'I saw none riding in. I couldn't swear they're all gone. We'll have to continue to be watchful.'

'Of course, but things will be better now?'

'Things will be better,' Ben told her firmly, and they turned to walk back to the house.

In the morning Ben told them sketchily what had happened as they sat at the breakfast table. Robin Stoker was too ill to come to the table, but he had an appetite, and that was something.

'To work on the spreader dam this morning?' Dink asked.

'Yes. With our rifles near at hand,' Ben agreed.

Ben was pleased with what he saw of the dam. The catch basin was nearly full already. The little pond behind the dam was spilling out at either end, allowing the tamed river to irrigate the parched land and the new grass there.

'Looks like we may as well start the second dam,

don't you think?' Dink asked. The young man stood beside Ben on the berm, holding his rifle with both hands. The rising breeze shifted his hair and tugged at his shirt. He looked somehow older, tougher on this morning.

Dink told him in a low voice, 'Today's my birthday, Ben. Eighteen at last.'

Ben Trout congratulated him. The two men shook hands and then got to work on the second dam they had planned. The day was long, very warm, the work hard, but they were beginning to see the results of their efforts. Once the black bull, Toro, wandered near to them, thinking unknown bull-thoughts, but they didn't bother to shoo him away. It would have been more trouble than it was worth, and eventually Toro decided that whatever the humans were up to was not worth his interest.

'How are you for a carpenter?' Dink asked as they rested on their tools.

'Me? I know up from down,' Ben answered with a self-disparaging laugh. 'Seriously, I can hang a joist, but I'm not sure I'd want to live in any house that I built.' He paused, squinting at Dink in the bright sunlight. 'Why do you ask?'

'It was Beth's thinking. Whenever you think it's safe to take the wagon into Riverton, she thought we should purchase some building materials, cement and lumber, and get started on Robin's house for him – seeing that he can't do it himself yet and his wife is on the way.

'Robin,' Dink continued, 'knows quite a bit about framing a house, as it turns out. He just can't swing a hammer himself yet. He could be kind of a supervisor while you and I did the rough work.'

'It'd be a break,' Ben shrugged. 'There's no hurry to finish this dam anyway as long as we've got the river managed.'

'What are you going to tell Beth?' Dink asked.

'I'm going to tell her that she's advancing her workers too much money, then do whatever the boss says.'

'She says that you're the boss, Ben.'

'Well, then, I will politely ask her to inform the boss what she would prefer that he do.'

'We'll be framing the house,' Dink said with a small grin.

'We'll be framing the house.'

THIRTEEN

Riverton was its same self two days later when Dink and Ben drove the wagon there to purchase building supplies with some more of Hiram Walsh's reward money, which Ben continually worried was getting eaten up at too rapid a pace. Five hundred dollars could dwindle away quickly if there was no income to replenish it.

They passed Marshal Charles Stout as they rolled toward the lumberyard, but the lawman did not hail them, although he did fix an uncertain look on Ben briefly. Halfway to the lumberyard, they passed the Overland Stage office. A small, uncertain woman stood in front of it, her trunks stacked beside her. She looked forlorn and lost.

'Dink! Slow this rig up. I think that woman is Cora Stoker.'

'I guess it could be. How many women take a

stagecoach to Riverton? I'll turn the wagon around, and we'll find out.'

Ben had guessed right. The woman turned out to be Cora Stoker. She was not what any of them had expected. Very small, almost tiny, she was nevertheless well proportioned and one of the most polite ladies Ben had met in his life. Soft-spoken, self-effacing, delicate in features and demeanor. She was a surprising contrast to the rugged Robin Stoker. And the little woman had braved the plains alone to come to her man! It was a lesson in the power of love.

They identified themselves as RU riders and offered her a ride to the ranch. It didn't seem the time to tell Cora that Robin was badly shot-up. That could wait until they were back at the ranch. Ben saw no harm in telling her that they were in town to pick up some lumber for the house that Robin was building for them to live in; in fact it seemed to raise Cora's spirits a little. She waited silently on the wagon seat while Ben and Dink loaded lumber purchased according to Robin's order.

'It'll be enough to throw up something before Cora gets here,' Robin had said, 'so that she sees a promise for the future.'

Things hadn't worked out quite like that, but Cora seemed far from disappointed.

Following the rough ride across the flat, open country, Ben drew up the team on the crest of the hills surrounding the RU and Cora broke out in a wreath of smiles. Below, the river and the ponds behind the spreader dams glinted brightly in the sunlight. The yard cows and Toro stood along the river with the range cattle that had drifted in once the water was restored. By the house Minna could be seen tending to her new vegetable garden, which chore she took inordinate pride in. The new grass was only a dusting of color across the dry land, but you could see where it was coming up.

'It's lovely,' Cora said in a tone which no one would have ever used about the RU even a few weeks ago.

'We have hopes,' Dink said. Then he pointed out the spot along the upper river where the small oak grove stood and where the land had already been leveled for Cora and Robin's new house. She thought it was perfect.

Pulling up in front of the house Cora was greeted by Beth and Minna and then taken inside. Ben and Dink left the lumber for later and started unloading Cora's trunks. After a lot of kissing and cautious hugging with which Cora and the wounded Robin reintroduced themselves to each other, Beth whisked Cora away to the back of the house to wash and change. The woman had been long on the road.

Robin stood like a thunderstruck man in the middle of the room, leaning on his crutch.

'Boys,' he said to Dink and Ben, 'you plan for things, you wish for them, but somehow you never really believe they will come true. And when it does happen – Lord, it feels fine!'

They tried to briefly discuss the framing of the new house with Robin, but it was futile. He was still off on his own, walking among the stars. In the end they just withdrew and hauled the lumber up to the home site and unloaded it, figuring that tomorrow was soon enough to do any more.

He came in the middle of the afternoon on the following day.

Why he was afoot was anybody's guess, but he walked directly toward the house as Ben Trout, ready to return to work after a quick dinner, stepped down from the porch.

'Hold it right there!' the stranger with the crooked mouth shouted angrily. 'I'm looking for Ben Trout.'

'I'm Ben Trout,' Ben answered, squinting into the sun to try to make out the features of the man who stood, hands curled at his side, dark hat tugged low over his eyes.

'My name's Aaron McCluskey. Trout, you've

caused me to lose out on a big payday. I had a con-
tract with Cyrus Sullivan. You killed him. I've come
for retribution.'

Looking at the man, knowing his reputation,
Ben knew that he wasn't going to talk McCluskey
out of it. He nodded and said, 'If you'll just let me
get my gun. . . .'

'You won't need one,' McCluskey said in a voice
which had faded from bitterness to simple
sarcasm. 'I'd beat you anyway – why waste all that
time?'

'So that I'd have a chance,' Ben said uneasily.
He didn't like the way things were shaping up.
McCluskey was wearing a confident smile now. He
wished that Dink had not stayed at the job site
while Ben ate, but then again he was glad that
Dink wouldn't be involved in this.

'I don't give chances,' McCluskey said. 'That's a
stupid way of doing business. When I shoot, I plan
to win.'

'You'd do murder, then?'

'Murder's just a word, Trout. Are you ready to
take it?'

No, he was not ready, but apparently he was
going to take it anyway. That was when the
booming blast from the porch sounded and before
McCluskey could draw his gun he was sent spin-
ning around, arms windmilling before he flopped

dead against the earth.

Ben turned to see Beth standing in front of the house, her big old Spencer .50-caliber buffalo gun leaking smoke from its muzzle.

'I had to. . . .' she said before she simply sat down on the porch, the rifle dropping free of her grip. 'He was going to. . . .'

'Yes, he was,' Ben said, also sitting, putting his arm around her to brace and caress her. Dink could be seen coming on the run from the river. He looked at the two people sitting on the porch and then walked to where the dead body lay sprawled.

Dink joked nervously, 'Well, we were wrong about that gun being enough to cut a man in half. He's still got a few threads holding him together.' Then Dink's false levity deserted him and he was forced to sit beside them on the porch. Minna had appeared from around the corner of the house in her gardening clothes, trowel in her hand. Her mouth opened to ask a question, but she looked at her mother's anguished face and simply went to sit down beside Dink to whisper to him.

Ben found that he was shaking only slightly less than Beth Robinson. 'That's as close as I ever want to come,' he said in a low voice. He managed to shake himself out of that dark mood and rise, calling to Dink, 'See that the tools are put away first, then go hitch the wagon and bring it around.'

'Are you going somewhere?' Beth asked.

'Have to,' Ben said, lifting his chin toward the dead man. 'We need to report this to Marshal Stout and deliver the body. There will be a reward coming, you know, Beth.'

'A reward?'

'Probably a quite large one. McCluskey was wanted in every county in West Texas.'

Beth nodded. There was no joy in her expression. 'What will Marshal Stout think of me?'

Dink had time for one more gibe before he left. 'He'll probably want to give you a badge and hire you on, the way you're cleaning up the outlaws in this part of the country.'

Beth couldn't even smile. Dink and Ben left the two women sitting on the porch close to one another for comfort and continued with disposing of Aaron McCluskey. Ben thought of McCluskey's words to him – 'Murder is just a word.' Now as he looked at the lifeless package of meat lying in the back of the wagon he couldn't help saying aloud: 'Dead is just a word. McCluskey.' Dink looked at him oddly, said nothing, and then started the wagon toward Riverton.

'How is the Stoker house coming along, Ben? I haven't had the chance to get up there.' Beth was

walking with Ben Trout in the late afternoon cool-
ness. They had chosen to make their way along the
top of the recently completed second spreader
dam. The pond water sparkled with rainbow
colors.

'Robin told us to hold off. He said he'd rather
finish the work himself. I don't know if that was
pride or a comment on our carpentry. He'll have it
finished in a week or ten days.'

'Did you know that Cora has already moved in
there? She told me that was the only place of her
own she has ever had, and she meant to stay. She
told me that she could sweep up sawdust as fast as
the men could make it, so that didn't concern
her.'

'It seems that they're planning on staying
around for a long time,' Ben said.

'It does . . . oh, look, Ben!' Beth said, pointing.
'Can that be what I think it is?'

She was looking at a walnut-sized chunk of
brightly glittering mineral mixed in with the material which formed the dam. They walked nearer.
Ben narrowed his eyes a little and then kicked the
stone off into the pond, where it rapidly sank.

'You must have been mistaken, Beth. I don't see
anything.'

'Neither do I now. You're right, I must have
been mistaken.'

Then, hand in hand, they walked back to the house in the light of dusk as the gold nugget was lost forever in the mud of the pond's bed.